"*The Girl on the Porch* had me hooked on page one—I devoured it. Chizmar peels the band-aid so slowly that it hurts...taut, deftly paced...we are all potentially guilty and anyone might die at any moment."

— CAROLINE KEPNES, BESTSELLING AUTHOR OF *YOU*

"Creepy as hell! A tense and twisty read that poses this unsettling question: How well do we know our friends and neighbors? In Richard Chizmar's world, the answer is more complicated—and frightening—than you think."

— RILEY SAGER, BESTSELLING AUTHOR OF *FINAL GIRLS*

"If Chizmar's goal here is to make you suspicious—and fearful—of everyone you know, including those closest to you, mission accomplished."

— LINWOOD BARCLAY

"With a pinch of *Blue Velvet* and a dash of "The Monsters Are Due on Maple Street," Chizmar's short sharp story of a terrified suburban neighborhood insightfully illuminates the fears and anxieties lying just beneath the surface of modern American life. *The Girl on the Porch* is a pitch perfect illustration of Hannah Arendt's maxim about the banality of evil."

— BENTLEY LITTLE

"Richard Chizmar writes clean, no-nonsense prose...sets his tales in no-nonsense, middle class neighborhoods I can relate to...and writes terrific stories served with a very large slice of Disquiet Pie."

— STEPHEN KING

"Richard Chizmar writes like a man who's been to hell and back and lived to tell its tales."

— CLIVE BARKER

T0035565

"*The Girl on the Porch* is a thrilling, page-turning delight. Richard Chizmar's voice is the magic; he pulls you in with the storytelling touch of an old friend, and this old friend takes you to some dark places. An all-too-plausible setup leads to an all-American nightmare. Don't miss this one!"

— MICHAEL KORYTA

"Chizmar's stories are hard-hitting, spooky, suspenseful, poignant, harrowing, heartbreaking and most of all very well-written. Excellent work!"

— ROBERT MCCAMMON

"Each tale…is a magic trick, luring you toward the light while leading you down an ever-darkening path. There is hope mingled with horror, and that's Chizmar's secret power. His storytelling always beats with a huge, passionate heart."

— *ENTERTAINMENT WEEKLY*

"Like Ray Bradbury, Richard Chizmar has a sweet, nostalgic streak. The past in his stories is always a warm, perfect place. The present, however, belongs more to Robert Bloch, as wonder gives way to horror. The twists are worthy of the old *Twilight Zone*. Enjoy."

— STEWART O'NAN

"Exceptional stories that lay our hearts, lives and fears bare with brutal, beautiful economy."

— MICHAEL MARSHALL SMITH

"Richard Chizmar's talent is a fierce, poignant marvel. His exquisite stories shatter."

— RICHARD CHRISTIAN MATHESON

"It's an idyllic little world Richard Chizmar has created. Boys fish in the shallows of a winding creek. A father tosses a baseball with his young son in the fading light of a summer day. There's the smell of fresh-cut grass. And then, well…just beneath the surface? There are those missing pets whose collars turn up in a shoebox. Or the disturbing photos the dead can leave behind. Or the terrible thing you might find yourself doing when a long lost brother suddenly returns, demanding money. Chizmar does a tremendous job of peeling back his world's shiny layers, revealing the rot that lies underneath. His stories feel like so many teeth: short and sharp and ready to draw blood."

— SCOTT SMITH

"Chilling and thought-provoking tales that quietly uncover horror in the most ordinary of lives."

— KELLEY ARMSTRONG

"Richard Chizmar has a very special talent for creating a homely, believable world—the kind of world that you and I live in every day. But he gradually invests that world with a creeping sense of unease, and then he throws open those suburban front doors and brings us face to face with all the unthinkable horrors that have been hiding behind them."

— GRAHAM MASTERTON

"Richard Chizmar will soon distinguish himself as a major writer of American suspense fiction."

— ED GORMAN

"Chizmar's *Girl On The Porch* packs a punch. Doorbell videos. Teens. Spooky neighbors. And a mystery not boiling under the surface but blazing in front of your eyes. I read it in one sitting with sweaty palms—just like one of the suspects in the novel. This guy can write! I felt like I was sitting around a campfire hearing a story. One that wouldn't let me sleep. One that would leave me pacing for hours afraid of the sound of my own footfalls."

— RIDLEY PEARSON

THE GIRL ON THE PORCH

THE GIRL ON THE PORCH

RICHARD CHIZMAR

CEMETERY DANCE PUBLICATIONS

Baltimore

❖ 2023 ❖

The Girl on the Porch
Copyright © 2019 by Richard Chizmar

All rights reserved. No part of this book may be reproduced in any form or by any electronic or mechanical means, including information storage and retrieval systems, without permission in writing from the publisher, except by a reviewer who may quote brief passages in a review.

Cemetery Dance Publications
132B Industry Lane, Unit #7
Forest Hill, MD 21050
www.cemeterydance.com

This book is a work of fiction. Names, characters, places and incidents either are products of the author's imagination or are used fictitiously. Any resemblance to actual events or locales or persons, living or dead, is entirely coincidental.

Cemetery Dance Trade Paperback Edition 2023

ISBN:
978-1-58767-882-0

Cover Artwork and Design © 2023 by François Vaillancourt
Interior Design © 2023 by Desert Isle Design, LLC

for Noah
King of the whodunits
with much love from your old man

FRIDAY

KENNY TUCKER smelled bacon frying as soon as he hit the stairs and by the time he walked into the kitchen, his stomach was growling up a storm.

Sarah, his wife of twenty-two years next month, stood at the counter, working the frying pan with one hand and tapping away at her cellphone with the other.

"Morning, sleepyhead," she said, smiling over her shoulder.

Kenny yawned and gave her a peck on the cheek, then sat down at the breakfast nook and took a sip of steaming coffee from the mug that was waiting for him there. He watched as Sarah cracked three eggs into a second frying pan, never once taking her eyes off her phone.

Barely five feet tall, dressed in yoga pants and t-shirt, long brown hair tied back in a ponytail, Sarah was a little ball of energy even at this early hour. Not to mention still beautiful after all these years. Kenny was a lucky man.

"What time did you finally get to bed?" she asked, picking up a spatula and scrambling the eggs.

He stifled another yawn. "Not sure, sometime after midnight I think."

She shook her head. "You're going to be walking around like a zombie at practice today."

"Not my fault the stupid kicker choked and the game went into overtime. At least the Steelers won this time." Kenny was a third generation Pittsburgh fan—hockey, baseball, but especially football—which meant he'd long ago learned to take the good with the bad. He rubbed his eyes. "Breakfast smells great, honey."

"Ready in two."

"Thanks. I can't be late today. I promised to help Tucker Benjamin with his essay before home room."

"Awfully nice of you." She slid several strips of crispy bacon onto a plate. "I have to wonder, though, if you'd be quite so eager to help if Tucker wasn't the starting tight end on the football team."

Kenny looked up from the newspaper he'd just started reading. "Hey, English teacher first, football coach second. You know that."

"Of course I do, silly. I was only teasing." She loaded up the plate with eggs and walked it over to the table and sat down across from her husband. "Poor baby. You get so sensitive when you're tired."

He took a big bite of scrambled eggs, chewed a couple times, and then opened his mouth wide, showing her his food.

She laughed. "You're disgusting."

"Natalie awake?" he asked, shoveling in another forkful.

"In the shower already. She said she wants to ride the bus today." Sarah got up from the table, walked back to the stove, and started pecking away on her phone again. "Dammit, how do you fast-forward this thing?" she muttered.

Kenny watched her for a moment. "What're you obsessing over? You usually avoid your cellphone like the plague this early in the morning. And God forbid if I'm on mine."

She looked up at him. "Angie texted. Someone rang their doorbell like ten times in the middle of the night last night. Woke up the whole house. When Frank finally dragged himself out of bed and checked the door, no one was there."

Angie and Frank Urban were their next-door neighbors. Good people, even if Angie was a little dramatic and gossipy for Kenny's taste. She was a great friend to Sarah, and that's all that really mattered.

"Probably a prank," he said. "We did that kind of stuff all the time when we were kids."

"In the middle of the night on a Thursday?"

"Hell, I can't remember what I did last week, much less thirty years ago. It was probably drunk college kids."

"Did you hear Bandit barking last night?"

Bandit was their three-year-old Corgi, currently guarding Sarah's vegetable garden in the back yard.

Kenny shook his head. "I didn't hear a thing once I turned off the television and hit the pillow. I was out."

She stared intently at the phone screen. "He woke me up around three-thirty. I figured he was stalking raccoons from the window again, didn't really think anything about it until this morning when I got Angie's text."

"You think he heard someone next door?"

"Maybe. Or maybe he heard someone at our house. You know the doorbell's been broken for months."

"I know, I know, it's on my list."

"I don't care about that, honey. It's the timing I'm curious about. Angie said it was just after three-thirty when Frank got back to bed. The same time Bandit started barking."

Kenny pushed away his empty plate. "Maybe he heard something next door. So what?"

"Got it!" she exclaimed, proudly holding out the phone to him.

"Got what?"

"Hear me out," she said, giving Kenny her full attention. "You know the little security camera you installed last year when packages started disappearing from front porches around the neighborhood?"

Kenny nodded. "Right around Thanksgiving."

"I've been trying all morning to figure out how to access last night's footage on my cellphone. I finally got it."

"What exactly is it that you're worried about, baby?"

Sarah shrugged. "I guess just the idea that someone might have been creeping around our house in the middle of the night. Remember a few months ago when Carly's friend noticed someone following her when she was jogging? That was pretty late at night and only two blocks away from here."

"I think you're being a little paranoid," he said, getting up from the table and dumping his dirty dishes into the sink.

Sarah sighed and went back to fast-forwarding the security footage. She slowed when the time code hit 3:28 a.m. and tapped the *Play* arrow. A grainy black-and-white image of their empty front porch appeared on screen.

Standing at the sink, Kenny stared at his reflection in the kitchen window and straightened his tie. "Tell Nat I said goodbye and we can all go out and get ice cream after—"

Sarah gasped.

He swung around to face her. "What's wrong?"

Eyes wide, she furiously tapped the screen, and angled the phone so he could see it. She nudged the *Play* arrow again with the tip of her finger. The same grainy image of their empty front porch appeared.

"Okay?" he said, confused.

"Just wait."

A few more seconds passed—

—and then a young woman hurried onto the porch and rang the doorbell. She was barefoot and dressed in an oversized t-shirt and underwear. Her hair was a mess of tangled knots. Some kind of restraint or shackle hung from her right wrist. The woman anxiously pressed the doorbell again and again, continually glancing over her shoulder at the front lawn and street as if she were terrified someone was coming for her. After twenty-three more seconds of this, the woman gave up and walked away from the door, still checking over her shoulder as she disappeared from view.

Sarah looked up at her husband. "Now what do you think?"

No longer half-asleep, he said, "I think Tucker Benjamin is going to have to write that essay all by himself this morning."

***

THE DETECTIVE'S NAME was Jenkins and Kenny found it nearly impossible not to stare because she looked exactly like his eighth grade art teacher, Mrs. Crabtree.

Mary Beth Crabtree, with her cheerful smile and southern accent and overflowing candy dish perched on the corner of her desk, had always been Kenny's favorite teacher. She had attended Kenny and Sarah's wedding, and they still exchanged emails and Christmas cards to this day. He couldn't get over the striking resemblance.

A lighter-skinned African American, a little on the plump side, with a scattering of freckles across her broad nose, and a deceptively soft lilt to her voice, Detective Jenkins sat in Kenny's well-used reading chair and scribbled away in her notepad while Kenny and Sarah sat opposite her on the sofa and did their best to answer her questions. They were both quite nervous.

The detective had arrived at the house almost an hour earlier. Right away, Kenny had noticed that she had what the writers whose books he taught in his modern lit classes would have called a "watchful gaze." Her eyes were everywhere and nowhere at once. He had no doubt she'd had the entire family room filed away in memory within minutes of taking a seat, right down to the brand and size of the television affixed to the wall above the fireplace, and the books and knickknacks sitting on the built-in shelves.

For the past several minutes, she'd been studying her notepad, slowly flipping from one page to the next and then back again, occasionally breaking the silence to follow up on a previous question. Sarah didn't know what made her feel more anxious: the long stretches of quiet or the repetitive questions that made her feel like the detective didn't believe a word they were saying.

"So…you said you moved here four years ago from Lancaster County?"

"That's right," Kenny said.

"And you commuted to your teaching job at Harford Day School before that?"

"No, I was working at a public school back then. Once I interviewed at Harford Day and signed a contract to teach and coach there, that's when we decided to move to Hanover."

She wrote something down and turned her attention to Sarah. "And you're not currently employed, is that right, Mrs. Tucker?"

"Not for the past eighteen months. I worked at Kernan Hospital as a physical therapist before that, but my father passed away in 2016 and left us some money." She glanced at Kenny, knowing she was babbling and wishing she could stop. "After that, my husband and I talked about it and we decided I should take some time off until Natalie graduated from high school. It's been wonderful, but I actually look forward to practicing again one day."

Another interminable stretch of silence—Sarah could hear the grandfather clock ticking away in the next room—and then:

"You're absolutely certain neither of you have ever seen the woman from the video before?"

"I'm sure," Sarah said.

Kenny nodded. "Me too."

"Not even in passing? The grocery store, the park, in the hallways at the hospital or school?"

"The video isn't very clear," Sarah said, trying to sound confident, "but I'm as sure as I can be."

This time Detective Jenkins didn't wait for a response from Kenny. "And your daughter..." She consulted her notes. "...Natalie, you'll show her the video when she gets home from school and let me know if she has anything to add?"

Kenny glanced nervously at his wife.

"We'll show her," he said. "Sarah's a little worried the video could frighten Natalie—she just turned thirteen and has a pretty wild imagination—but if you think it's important, we'll ask her to watch and get back to you."

"I'd appreciate that," the detective said, looking down at her notepad again.

"Will the police be conducting a house-to-house search in the neighborhood?" Sarah asked.

"Nothing quite so drastic, but we already have officers questioning many of your neighbors, and my partner is next door as we speak interviewing your friends, the Urbans. Keep in mind, Mrs. Tucker, we don't actually know if the woman in the video came from a nearby house. She may have escaped from a car traveling through the area or even been dumped here. Or...the whole thing could just be some sort of misunderstanding."

"A misunderstanding," Sarah repeated.

"Oh, you'd be surprised at the things we come across, even out here in the suburbs. That's why it's important that we make the video available to the public as soon as possible via the local news and social media. Someone might recognize her or perhaps the woman herself will see it and come forward to straighten out what happened."

"Absolutely," Kenny said. "Feel free to share it wherever you'd like."

Detective Jenkins flipped to another page. "You mentioned your neighbor across the street earlier, Tom Carpenter. Anything else you can add to what you've already told me?"

"Not really," Kenny said. "Tom keeps to himself most of the time. I know he works at a bank somewhere downtown, not sure which one. Other than that, he's quiet, doesn't really have a lot of visitors. The only reason I mentioned him at all is because you asked if I knew of any single people who lived nearby. He's the only one I can think of, besides Paul next door and the woman who—"

"That would be Paul Blauner?" the detective asked, checking her notes.

"Yes. Wonderful guy. Used to be a city cop. His wife passed away from cancer the year before we moved in. He's in his mid-seventies and has become a kind of father figure to Sarah and me. Our daughter adores him."

"And you mentioned a woman?"

"Keri something. I told you about her before. She moved into the big house on the corner last month. But the rumor mill…" Kenny hooked a thumb in Sarah's direction. "…has it on good authority that she's engaged to some big-wig law-yer and they're already living together."

Sarah swatted Kenny on the leg and laughed uneas-ily. "Paul's a sweetheart and Tom Carpenter's a nice guy," she said. "I'm sure neither one had anything to do with the woman on our porch."

Detective Jenkins looked up from her notes, surprising Sarah with the intensity of her gaze.

"You know, Mrs. Tucker, if your hair was just a tad shorter, you'd look a lot like our mysterious doorbell ringer."

Sarah forced herself to meet the detective's eyes. "You really think so?"

Nodding her head. "I really do."

Kenny studied his wife and shrugged. "I'm sorry. I don't see it."

"No reason to be sorry." She flipped a page in her note-book, traced a couple of sentences with her finger, and then flipped back to where she had started. "Just one final ques-tion, and I'm sorry to keep asking you this, Mr. Tucker, but I need you to be one hundred percent certain."

"Okay."

"You're sure you've never seen the woman on the video before? Anywhere and at any time in your life?"

Kenny could feel Sarah's eyes on him as he shook his head. He was starting to sweat. *Why in the hell didn't the detective believe him?* "I'm sure, Detective. I've never laid eyes on the woman."

Detective Jenkins snapped her notebook closed and got to her feet. "In that case, I'll get out of your hair." She started for the front door. "Please let me know what your daughter has to say after she's had a chance to watch the video."

"Will do," Kenny said, relieved that it was over.

Sarah walked her out.

~

"TRUST ME, I'VE talked to pretty much everyone on the block," Angie said. "It was only our two houses. It's like she appeared out of nowhere and then just disappeared into thin air."

Even dressed in faded jeans and a Penn State baseball cap, Angie Urban looked put-together. Like an actress in an afternoon soap opera or a rich housewife in one of those reality shows. Her silver earrings complimented her necklace and her necklace complimented her bracelets—all of which combined to highlight the trendy, studded belt she was wearing. Her make-up, as usual, was perfection.

"Or maybe our two houses were all she had time to try before someone came along and snatched her away," Sarah said.

They were sitting in the old-fashioned rockers on Angie's wrap-around front porch. Drinking hot tea and catching each other up on the latest news. Both of their cellphones were buzzing with incoming texts and voice mails from curious friends, most of which they ignored.

Once Detective Jenkins left, Kenny grabbed a light lunch and headed in for the second half of the school day. The football team had a bye this weekend, but they were putting in a series of new plays at practice today in preparation for next Saturday's game and he didn't want to miss it.

Sarah had waited not very patiently—pacing back and forth on her own front porch—for Jenkins's partner, Detective Giambanco, to finish interviewing Frank and Angie, and as soon as the unmarked sedan had pulled away from the curb, she'd scampered right over there.

Angie grimaced. "I can't even think about that. I feel guilty enough as it is."

"You and me both," Sarah said. "That poor woman."

"At least you guys have an excuse. You never heard a thing. We heard the doorbell and still didn't help."

"But you tried." Sarah patted her friend's leg. "That's what counts."

"If Frank wasn't so damn slow..."

A black SUV turned the corner and slowed down in front of the house.

"Anyone we know?" Sarah asked, stretching to get a better look.

"Don't think so."

The SUV sped up again and disappeared down the street.

Sarah shivered. "This whole thing gives me the creeps. I'm almost afraid to go to sleep tonight."

"I said the same thing to Frank."

"What did he say?"

"What do you think he said?" Imitating Frank's deep voice: "'Stop being such a baby, Ang. The neighborhood's never been safer than it is right now thanks to all the attention. Police walking around asking questions during the day, extra patrols at night.'"

"I never thought of that," Sarah said. "Speaking of cops, how was your detective?"

Angie smiled. "He was actually kinda cute."

"Oh my God, that's not what I meant."

She laughed. "Well, I swore to tell the truth, the whole truth, and nothing but the truth."

Sarah shook her head. "You're a piece of work."

"The detective was fine," Angie said, waving a hand dismissively. "Asked a handful of questions and went on his merry way."

"Same with ours, but she was a little more…"

Angie looked at her friend. "What?"

"I don't know. She asked a lot of the same questions over and over again, each time in a slightly different way. Like she didn't believe us or was trying to catch us in a lie or something."

"I've seen detectives do that on television. It's just how they do their jobs."

"Did Detective Giambanco act that way with you guys?"

Angie thought about it for a moment. "Not really."

"See, that doesn't make me feel better."

"You're just being paranoid," Angie said, standing up and stretching. "I wouldn't worry about it."

"Easy for you to say."

"I need to get inside and start getting ready for dinner." She made a face. "Frank's parents are coming over tonight."

"Oh, joy. Good luck with that." Sarah stood and started off the porch.

"One more thing," Angie said.

Sarah turned back to her friend.

"Detective Giambanco? He really did have the tightest little ass on him."

"Piece. Of. Work," Sarah said, and walked home, laughing.

***

KENNY FINISHED GARGLING and spit the mint-flavored mouthwash into the sink. He turned off the bathroom light and crawled into bed next to his wife. She closed the paperback she was reading.

"Natalie was pretty quiet tonight, don't you think?" she asked.

"I would say she was…thoughtful. That video's a lot to process for only being thirty seconds long."

"You're telling me." Sarah hesitated, and then went on. "There's a part of me that's really angry with Detective Jenkins for asking us to do that. She's only a kid."

Kenny nestled his head on his wife's shoulder. "She's just doing her job, honey."

"That's what Angie said."

"Make sure you mark that on the calendar. October fifth. Kenny and Angie agree on something."

Sarah giggled. "Smart ass."

"I left the detective a message when I took Bandit out to pee. Let her know Natalie didn't recognize the woman."

"Which is exactly what we told her would happen."

"I also double-checked the deadbolt like you asked me to."

"Thank you, baby." Sarah turned her head and kissed him on the cheek. "Can I ask you just one more favor?"

"Of course."

"Would you mind looking out the bedroom window?"

"Right now?"

"If you don't mind."

Kenny peeled off the sheet and climbed out of bed. "What exactly am I looking for?"

"I don't know. Anything…out of the ordinary, I guess."

He walked over to the window. Used a finger to part the curtains.

The front lawn and street beyond were lost in a spider-web of shadows. A fingernail sliver of October moon hung high in the night sky. There was no breeze. Nothing stirred, not even the tree branches.

"Everything looks fine," he said, returning to bed.

"Thank you for checking." She slid her paperback onto the nightstand. "I can't stop thinking about her. I keep seeing her face. She looked so scared."

Kenny turned off the bedside lamp. "Try to get some sleep. Tomorrow will be a better day, I promise."

A whisper in the darkness: "Kenny?"

"Yeah, babe."

"You've really never seen that woman before?"

He rolled over to face his wife. "Never. You heard what I told the detective."

"But it's *me* asking you this time. You're sure?"

Kenny reached out in the dark and found his wife's hand. "Yes, honey. I'm sure."

"I love you."

"I love you back."

It was a long time before either of them found sleep.

THE MAN WAS about to leave his hiding place behind the old oak tree when someone appeared in the upstairs window of the house he was watching. He immediately shrunk back into the shadows.

The man recognized the face in the window. He watched as the person stood there for a moment, staring out at the night, and then the curtains closed again. A short time later, the light in the window went dark.

The man watched the house for several minutes longer. Once he was convinced it was safe, he crawled out from behind the tree and cut his way through a pair of pitch-dark back yards, hopping fences and narrowly avoiding a birdbath and goldfish pond, before emerging on the deserted side-street where he'd left his car.

SATURDAY

MOWING THE lawn was one of Kenny Tucker's great pleasures in life. He liked nothing more on a Saturday morning than to gas up the John Deere, slip on headphones, crank up some classic rock, and off he'd go. Something about cutting all those sharp-edged lines into the lush grass—horizontal one week, vertical the next—appealed to the meticulous side of his brain. It was also relaxing. Once a week, for at least ninety minutes, he didn't have to worry about three-four defenses, double tight end sets, or keeping his best players eligible for the playoffs.

Today was a perfect example. It wasn't even ten o'clock yet, and Sarah and Angie were already huddled around the kitchen table drinking coffee and fussing over the mysterious woman from the video. And it seemed like half of the neighborhood was doing much of the same. No fewer than three of Kenny's neighbors had stopped by earlier in the morning while he'd been busy edging the driveway and sidewalk, all of them asking a variation of the same breathless question: *Have the police found out anything yet?*

Kenny had never been in more of a hurry to fire up the mower, slip on his headphones, and shut out the rest of the world. Sure, he was curious about the woman and concerned for her well-being, but there wasn't a whole lot he could do about it at this point. He'd talked to the detective and handed over the security footage—what else could he do?

He guided the mower down the narrow strip of side yard, careful not to disturb the flowerbed Sarah had planted alongside the garage, and when he reached the split-rail fence that encircled his half-acre back yard, Kenny pivoted and steered back toward the street—where his next-door neighbor, Paul Blauner, was waiting for him on the sidewalk.

Kenny smiled—genuinely happy to see his friend—and hit the *Kill* switch on the John Deere. The growl of the mower's engine went silent and was replaced by the comforting sounds of the neighborhood: a dog barking somewhere down the street; the rhythmic slap of a basketball on pavement; shouts of excitement from a kids' backyard whiffle ball game.

"Just the man I wanted to see," Kenny said, shaking his neighbor's hand.

Paul Blauner was in his mid-seventies but could have passed for twenty years younger. He still had a full head of thick gray hair and his biceps were bigger than Kenny's. He walked two miles every evening and did an every-other-day regimen of sit-ups and push-ups.

"I was going to stop by earlier," Paul said. "But I saw you had company. Figured I'd wait until you were finished mowing anyway."

"It was like a damn parade out here this morning."

Paul nodded. "I saw Ronnie Washington ambush you from my kitchen window."

Kenny rolled his eyes. "Every time I think the guy can't get any sleazier, he proves me wrong."

"What'd he do this time?"

"Nothing he did, something he *said*. About the woman on the video."

"Of course," Paul sighed.

"Sarah told me the police talked to you yesterday. I was going to come over after practice last night, but the detective asked us to show Natalie the video just in case she recognized the woman."

Paul cringed a little. "How'd that go?"

"Okay, I guess. She seemed more confused than anything."

"She doesn't know about that part of the world yet. Unfortunately, it's just a matter of time."

"Sarah wasn't happy."

"I bet," Paul said. "I'll talk to her. Explain how these sort of investigations tend to operate."

"You ever have a case like this when you were working in the city?"

"Not exactly, but close enough. Not much we didn't see."

"How'd they usually turn out for you?"

Paul shook his head and looked at the ground. "Not good."

A young boy whizzed by on a skateboard, startling them. "Hey, Mr. Tucker. Hey, Mr. Blauner."

Both men waved. "Slow down, Tommy!" Kenny shouted after him, but the boy was already gone.

"Ah, to be young and foolish again," Paul said, staring wistfully down the street.

"Speaking of fools, me and the boys are playing poker tonight. You want to join us?"

"Thanks, but I'll probably be crawling into bed about the time you fellows are dealing the first hand."

"If you change your mind, you know you're welcome."

"Appreciate that, Ken."

Kenny looked at the grass-covered mower. "I guess I better get this thing cleaned up and back in the garage. Sarah has a busy rest of the day planned for me."

"Stop by later if you get a break," Paul said, waving and heading for his house.

"Thanks. I might do that."

Just as he reached the sidewalk, Paul stopped and turned back to his neighbor. "Ken?"

Kenny looked up. "Yeah?"

"I was wondering...did Natalie recognize the woman in the video?"

He shook his head. "Never seen her before. Just like the rest of us."

"Figured as much," Paul said and walked the rest of the way home.

ssh

"KENNY!"

"I'm coming," he said, hurrying down the stairs and into the family room. "Sorry to keep you guys waiting. I had to get—"

Sarah *ssshed* him and turned up the volume on the television.

The perky blonde newscaster from Channel Eleven was sitting behind an anchor desk. A black-and-white screenshot of the woman from the video dominated the upper right corner of the shot. A banner headline running along the bottom of the screen read: **LOCAL POLICE INVESTIGATING SUSPICIOUS INCIDENT IN HANOVER.**

"Holy shit," Kenny said.

As the reporter launched into her story, the screenshot was replaced by an enlarged image of the woman's face:

"On October fourth at approximately 3:30 a.m., a resident of the Broadview Acres subdivision in Hanover was awakened by a ringing doorbell. By the time the homeowner went downstairs and answered the door no one was there. While reviewing

their video surveillance system the next morning they observed the following footage…"

A short clip of the video began to play.

"The Hanover County Sheriff's Office was alerted and is currently investigating the suspicious incident. Deputies confirm there are no missing persons reports from the area that match this individual. Deputies and detectives have canvassed the neighborhood and completed door-to-door interviews of residences as well as businesses in the area. Deputies are also reviewing video surveillance from surrounding residences and businesses."

A phone number and email address appeared at the bottom of the television screen.

"If you recognize the woman in this video or if you are the woman in this video, please contact the Hanover County Sheriff's Office at 717-232-1515. You can also email hsomedia@rcpa.org."

Sarah muted the television and turned to her husband. "Wow."

"They didn't even get the story right," Kenny said.

Sarah was about to respond when Natalie bopped into the room wearing headphones. "I'm starving," she said, about ten times louder than necessary. "We going to dinner or what?"

"PHONE," KENNY SAID, motioning for his daughter to put it away.

The teenager pouted and slid the cellphone back into her pocket. The restaurant was crowded, even for a Saturday evening, and their orders were taking forever. All three of them were hungry and cranky.

"What are we supposed to do until the food comes?" Natalie whined.

"Heaven forbid we actually talk to each other," Sarah said.

"What's so important that it can't wait until after dinner anyway?" Kenny asked, trying to lighten the mood. "Must be a *boyyy*."

Natalie rolled her eyes at her father. "It's not a boy, Dad. It's Krissy and Madison and Taylor. They've been texting about the video all day."

"What about the video?" Sarah asked.

"It's all over social media. We're practically famous."

Sarah glanced anxiously at her husband.

He shrugged. "We knew this was going to happen."

"What are your friends saying?" Sarah asked.

"Well, Krissy said she thinks the woman escaped from a serial killer and she's safe and sound with the police, but they're not telling anyone because they're going to use her as bait to catch the guy. Taylor thinks the woman escaped from an abusive husband, but the husband found her and has her chained up in the attic again."

"Oh, really," Sarah said, looking none too pleased. "And what does Madison have to say?"

"She thinks the woman is from outer space."

"What?" Kenny asked, stifling a laugh.

Natalie shrugged. "Madison says the woman is an alien who escaped from a spaceship, but they captured her and beamed her back up."

"Where do you kids get this stuff?" Kenny said.

"I don't think it's appropriate to joke about any of this," Sarah said, with an edge to her voice. "We're talking about this poor woman's life."

"We weren't joking," Natalie said, looking down at the table.

"Well, how about you girls change the subject to something a little more cheerful?" Sarah said.

"I'll try but they're pretty excited about it."

Sarah's face darkened and she was about to admonish the girl further when the waitress arrived with their dinner. "I apologize for the wait, folks. The kitchen's a mess tonight."

"Saved by the bell," Kenny said, smiling.

While the waitress served Sarah her lasagna and garlic bread, Kenny noticed a man standing at the bar staring at them. He was short and muscular like the wrestlers Kenny hung around with in college. His hair was cropped close and his nose looked like it had been broken more than once. Kenny met his unwavering stare, but the man refused to look away.

The waitress leaned over to serve Natalie a plate of stuffed shrimp and pasta, momentarily blocking Kenny's view. When she moved out of the way, the man at the bar was gone.

***

"THE NAME OF the game is Forty-Four, deuces wild," Kenny said, dealing the cards.

The other four men sitting around the poker table groaned. Three of them lived in the same development as Kenny: Ian Warrick (two streets over), Trey Whiteford (their back yards practically abutted), and David Blessing (a block away). The fifth player, Craig Anderson, lived in nearby Edgewood. Longtime friends, they'd played poker on the first Saturday night of every month for going on five years now, rotating hosting duties each time. Tonight's game was at Trey's house.

"Oh, goodie, more prison poker," David said.

"What do you have against wild cards?" Kenny asked.

"If I wanted to play with wild cards, I would've stayed home and played Uno with my kids."

"Christ, can I get one decent hand?" Craig said, looking at his cards. "Is that too much to ask?"

"I bet a buck," Ian said, tossing in a red chip and drinking from his beer.

The table was a mess of playing cards, poker chips—Ian's stack was the highest so far, but the night was young—and empty beer bottles. A single can of soda sat next to Kenny's small pile of chips. A barely touched bowl of pretzels rested at one end of the table, an identical bowl of cashews at the other end.

"I'm out," David said, tossing his cards in the pot.

Craig fake-coughed in his fist. "Pussy."

"You play my cards, see what happens," David said, face flushing red.

The other men laughed. Craig loved getting in David's head. It was even more entertaining on the golf course.

"Pot is right," Kenny said and flipped over the first of four down-cards: ten of clubs.

"Still my bet," Ian said. "I'll go another buck."

"I'm in," Craig said, tossing in a chip.

"Not me," said Trey, turning over his cards.

Kenny slid a chip into the pot. "Here we go." He flipped over another card: jack of spades.

"Buck," Ian said.

"I'm done." Craig pushed his cards to the center of the table.

"I'll see one more," Kenny said. He slid a chip into the pot and turned over a third card: seven of hearts.

"Ugly fucking draw," David said.

"You're an ugly fucking draw," Craig said.

David scowled at him. "That doesn't even make any sense."

"Staying with a buck," Ian said.

Kenny matched him and turned over the final down-card: ten of spades.

"Someone's holding a ten," Craig said, looking back and forth between Kenny and Ian.

"A buck," Ian said, tossing in another red chip.

"Raise one," Kenny said, rolling in a black chip.

"And now we know who it is," Craig said, grinning at Kenny.

Ian studied his friend, looking for a tell. "You sneaky bastard, you bluffing again?"

"Pay your dollar and find out."

Ian picked up a chip, hesitated, and then nudged it into the pot. "Call."

Kenny turned over his cards. "Four tens."

Trey whistled.

"Jesus," David said.

Ian flung his cards across the table. "Lucky motherfucker."

"Pure skill, my friend. Pure skill." Kenny smiled and raked the pot.

Craig got up from the table. "Gotta take a piss, deal me out." He disappeared into the hallway.

"We'll wait for you," Ian said, collecting the cards.

"Grab me a Sprite from the fridge when you come back," Kenny called after him.

"You guys hear about Ian's latest stalker?" Trey asked.

Ian was an orthodontist with a successful practice out past the mall. Handsome, in shape, and more stylish than the other four men combined, he was the frequent target of "mom crushes" at his office.

"Spill it," Kenny said.

"Not much to it," Ian said. "She friended me on Facebook and now she won't leave me alone. Sends messages and pictures every day."

"What kind of pictures?" David asked.

Ian took a drink of his beer. "The highly inappropriate kind."

"So why don't you block her?" Trey asked.

"She has three kids," Ian said, smiling that shark grin of his. "And they all need braces."

The men laughed.

"Wish I had that kind of problem at work," David said.

Kenny rolled his eyes. "Here we go."

David sold insurance with his father. His complaints regarding his career path were legendary within the group.

He looked at the other men. "I'm just saying. It's boring as hell."

"Oh, we know what you're saying all right," Ian said and quickly tried to change the subject. "How about you, Trey? How's the real estate biz?"

He shrugged. "Business is steady. I can't complain."

"You sell the Wilkerson place yet?" Kenny asked.

"I wish. Six months on the market and not even a sniff."

"Why not?"

"Too old. Too out of the way. Too expensive. I tried to talk Wilkerson into dropping it another thirty grand, but the stubborn bastard won't do it. He just sits in that nursing home counting his money all day."

"You'd think he'd be anxious to sell," David said. "My father says he's almost ninety."

"Who'd be anxious to sell?" Craig asked, walking into the room. He handed Kenny a cold can of Sprite.

"Old man Wilkerson," Ian answered. "We were just swapping work stories."

"Not that you'd know anything about work," Kenny said.

"Hey now," Trey said. "I'm sure it's not easy playing thirty-six holes in an afternoon. Even with a cart."

"Ha, ha, very funny," he said, taking his seat at the table. Craig was the assistant golf pro at Mountain Branch Country Club in Edgewood. The other guys never passed up an opportunity to remind him that he essentially got paid to play a game.

"I have an idea," David said suddenly.

The other four men looked at him.

He cleared his throat. "You know how some neighborhoods have a citizen patrol? Kind of like a neighborhood watch program?"

"Sure," Ian said. The others nodded their agreement.

"I was thinking…maybe we should try it. Not like as a regular thing, just a couple of nights."

"Why us?" Trey asked.

"Why not us?" David said. "Between the five of us, we know half the people in town. And we definitely know the neighborhood."

"What do you hope to accomplish?" Craig asked. "It's not like we're in the midst of a crime spree or something."

"He's thinking about the woman in the video," Kenny said, and all eyes turned to him.

David nodded. "When we talked about it earlier, we pretty much all agreed that she had to escape from some-where nearby. She was half-naked and barefoot. So where? Who lives alone and could have done something like this? Has to be a loner, unless the wife was in on it, too. And, if that was the case, they most likely don't have kids."

"I know you're bored at work," Trey said. "But this is kinda looney, even for you, David."

"Maybe not," Ian said.

The men looked at him in surprise.

"Think about it. Someone had that poor woman locked up inside their house. Maybe someone we all know. Maybe someone we see and talk to every day. What would it hurt to walk around the neighborhood a couple of nights? Keep our eyes open and see if we can spot anything out of the ordinary."

"I thought the police were looking at the guy across the street from you," Craig said to Kenny.

"Tom Carpenter? Where did you hear that from?"

"I thought he was gay," Trey said.

Kenny threw his hands up. "I have no idea if he's gay and no idea who the police are looking at."

"I still think you're holding out on us," David said.

"Okay, so it's settled," Ian said, looking around the table. "We're all in."

"We are?" Trey asked, looking at Kenny.

Kenny shrugged and took a drink of Sprite.

"Date and time to be determined," Ian said and started dealing the cards.

"YOU FINISH UP or down?" Ian asked, holding the front door open.

"Think I'm even," Kenny said. "Give or take five bucks. You?"

Ian closed the door behind them, and they walked across the lawn to their cars.

"Up around ninety."

Kenny whistled. "Good for you."

Ian checked his wristwatch. "Where was David in such a hurry to get to anyway?"

"Where else? Home, I'm sure."

Ian stopped walking. "Hey, listen, if you'd rather we didn't do that whole neighborhood watch thing, I'd understand. I'll call the guys off."

Kenny thought about it for a moment. "Nah, it's fine. It's just been kind of strange, especially since the video was released. Sarah's really torn up about it."

"Let me know if you change your mind."

"Thanks, I'll—"

A metallic clanging sound came from somewhere in the darkness across the street.

Both men turned and stared.

"What was that?" Ian asked, clearly spooked.

Kenny took a couple steps into the road and tried to get a better look. "Sounded like someone knocked over a trash can or banged against the siding of a house."

"Probably a cat."

"Must've been a big cat."

"Want to go check it out?"

Kenny looked at his friend. "Hell, no. Do you?"

"Hell, no," Ian said, smiling now.

They stood there and listened for another minute to hear if the sound returned. When it didn't, they said goodnight and got in their cars and drove away.

SUNDAY

LMOST OVERNIGHT, she had become known as "The Girl on the Porch"—and she was everywhere. News coverage on all three local networks, pick-up stories on CNN and Fox News, viral posts on all the big social media platforms, and scores of flyers with her face plastered on telephone poles, road signs, and storefront windows all across the county. You couldn't run into a grocery store or pick up a burger and fries at a fast-food drive-thru without seeing the mystery woman's face staring back at you. Kenny and Sarah figured it was only a matter of time before someone recognized her and stepped forward.

✺

KENNY TURNED THE corner and picked up his pace. He knew it was a quarter mile from the fire hydrant he'd just passed to the front edge of his driveway. He usually sprinted this final leg of his morning run if he had any gas left in the tank.

Today wasn't one of those days, though.

He was dragging. He slowed down and coasted the final hundred or so yards. *Too much junk food and not enough sleep,* he thought, stretching his calves on the curb in front of his house.

He heard a car engine start nearby and looked up.

Tom Carpenter was backing out of his driveway. He swung onto the road and gave Kenny a friendly wave before putting the car in gear and driving away.

Kenny smiled and returned the wave—and felt horrible. He remembered what Craig had said the night before at poker and realized that if the detectives really were checking out Tom, it was probably on the basis of Kenny's own words.

Me and my big mouth, he thought, heading toward the garage. Sarah was right. Tom was a nice guy. Since when had being quiet and keeping to yourself been grounds for suspicion?

"Bet you a hundred bucks he's involved somehow."

Kenny looked up, startled.

Frank Urban stood in his side yard, leaning on a garden rake. He was wearing a too-tight tank top and jean shorts. His fleshy shoulders and cheeks were already turning pink from too much sun.

"Jesus, I didn't see you there, Frank."

"Sorry 'bout that. Everyone's a little jumpy these days."

"What was that you said?" Kenny asked, even though he was pretty sure he'd heard him correctly the first time.

Frank gestured across the street. "I said I bet you a hundred dollars that weirdo's involved with our mystery lady."

So now she's our *mystery lady,* Kenny thought.

"Why do you think that?" he said coolly.

"Who else could it be?" Frank said, lowering his voice and looking around conspiratorially. He held up a fist and extended a meaty finger every time he rattled off a nugget of investigatory wisdom: "The guy lives alone. Doesn't talk to anyone. Never has any visitors. The chick shows up directly across the street from his house. And no one hears a car drive in or out around the time she appeared." Frank waved all five fingers in Kenny's face. "That's too many goddam coincidences for it to be anything else. It's gotta be him."

All of a sudden, Kenny felt exhausted—and irritable. He found that he couldn't think of a single civil thing to say to his next-door neighbor, and then gratefully he didn't have to.

"Ken, can you give me a hand?" Sarah called out from behind the house.

"Gotta go," he said, breathing a sigh of relief as he pushed open the gate and latched it behind him. "Catch you later, Frank."

~~~

SARAH COULD SEE her husband standing by the garage talking to Frank Urban from where she was kneeling in front of her vegetable garden. She couldn't hear what they were saying, but she guessed it was about the woman from the video. It was all anyone was talking about these days.

She pulled another clump of weeds and tossed it onto the pile she had started next to her in the grass. Usually, by this time of year, her garden would be shriveled and dying, but with the excessively hot and rainy summer they'd had, her little patch of homegrown vegetables was still hanging on. She scooted over and was about to begin on a new section when she noticed the footprints.

Her arms broke out in gooseflesh.

There, in a patch of dark soil separating her tomatoes from her cucumbers, was a staggered line of clearly defined footprints. They were large and there were five of them. *They're definitely not mine,* she thought, her head swirling. *They're not Kenny's either. He knows better than to mess around in my garden. So whose are they?*

She tried to remember the last time she had worked in the garden. It had been a long week even before the mysterious woman had showed up on their porch—with Natalie being home sick from school the first two days and then the washing machine breaking down—and she was having trouble pinpointing the exact day.

And then it came to her: she had gone into the back yard and picked a handful of tomatoes on Friday afternoon after the detective had left, not long before she'd walked next door and talked to Angie. Kenny had grilled steaks later that night for dinner and she'd made baked potatoes and a big bowl of fresh salad. They'd eaten outside on the patio. If the footprints had been in the garden on Friday afternoon, she would have noticed them. She was certain of it.

Which meant someone had been creeping around their back yard *after* that Friday afternoon...*after* the mysterious woman had appeared on their porch and rang the doorbell... and *after* she had disappeared without a trace.

Was someone watching them? Even now?

She shivered, despite the warm sunshine, and scanned the line of trees that marked the rear of their property. Dark pools of shadow stared back at her. After a short time, her eyes returned to the footprints and she called out to her husband.

"WHAT DO YOU think?" Sarah asked. "Should we call the detective?"

Kenny stared down at the footprints. "You're sure they weren't already here?"

She nodded. "Absolutely positive."

"Did any of the detectives or police officers come out back?"

"I was with you the whole time, but I don't think so."

Kenny frowned. "Why would anyone want to sneak around and spy on us? Even if it's somehow related to that woman, it's public knowledge we didn't open the door. We never saw or spoke to her."

"Don't remind me," Sarah said.

"I'm going to get my cellphone and take some pictures," Kenny said. "Just in case."

"In case of what?" Sarah asked, and then she was clutching his arm, hard, and frantically pointing toward the back gate.

A man was standing there watching them.

"Hey!" Kenny called out, breaking into a jog. "Can I help you with something?"

The man waited until Kenny got closer and then he held up a laminated identification card with his photo in the upper right-hand corner. "Mark Bruce. *Hanover Herald*. I was wondering if you and your wife would mind answering a couple questions."

"Hell, yes, we mind," Kenny said in a loud voice. "This is private property." He swung open the gate.

"I understand that," the reporter said, backing up and nervously adjusting his glasses. "But your video has gotten a lot of attention in a very short amount of time and our readers would love to hear what you have to say about it."

"We already told everything we know to the police," Kenny said. He spotted a silver compact car parked at the curb that he assumed belonged to their uninvited guest and started toward it. The reporter struggled to keep up with him.

"Please. Just five minutes, Mr. Tucker?"

"No, thanks."

"Three minutes?"

Kenny looked closely at the reporter. The guy was practically a kid. He didn't even look like he shaved yet. "How'd you find out where we lived?"

He shrugged. "Your street name is listed in the Media Advisory that went out with the video. After watching it five or six times, it was pretty easy to match up the footage with your front porch."

"So you've been driving up and down the street all morning looking for our house?"

"It actually only took about ten minutes," he said, looking embarrassed.

Kenny stopped and put a hand on the younger man's shoulder. "Tell me the truth, have you been snooping around in our back yard?"

The reporter looked mortified. "No way. I swear. I would never do that."

Kenny believed him. He started walking again.

"People have a lot of questions after watching the video, Mr. Tucker."

From behind them: "What kind of questions?"

The two men stopped and turned around.

"What kind of questions?" Sarah repeated levelly.

"Well, Mrs. Tucker, for one: Why didn't you open the door?"

"Doorbell's broken," Kenny snapped. "We never heard a thing."

The young reporter nodded. "Okay, that's just the sort of thing I was talking about. That's good to know."

"What else?" Sarah asked.

Mark Bruce, of the *Hanover Herald*, eighteen months out of journalism school and making just enough to afford a roach-infested, one-bedroom apartment out by the airport, summoned the remainder of his courage and said, "The woman on the video hasn't been seen or heard from again. Do you feel guilty for not helping her? Do you feel responsible for whatever has happened to her?"

Sarah's chin began to tremble, and she suddenly burst into tears.

"Okay, that's enough," Kenny said, grabbing the reporter by the elbow and dragging him toward the curb. He yanked open the driver's door and shoved the man inside. Standing there in the middle of the road, hands on his hips, he glared at the car until it disappeared around the corner.

By the time he returned to Sarah, she was sitting in the grass, face buried in her hands, sobbing.

SARAH TOOK ANOTHER sip of wine and watched the squirrels chase each other across the back yard. It was her third glass of cabernet—she'd had two with dinner—and she had a nice buzz going. She was finally starting to relax.

The reporter had upset her with his abrupt appearance and blunt questions, but it had been more than that. Like some kind of sadistic mind-reader, he'd cut right to the heart of the matter and zeroed in on Sarah's most vulnerable emotion: guilt.

She'd wanted to scream at the reporter: "Yes, as a matter of fact, I *do* feel guilty for not helping that woman! I *do* feel responsible!" But she hadn't been able to get a single word out. Instead, it'd felt like her entire body had been paralyzed by his question—by his giving her deepest, innermost thoughts and fears a voice.

Like a child, she'd sobbed in Kenny's arms and allowed him to lead her inside the house and put her to bed for a nap. She'd fallen asleep with an endless loop of pointless admonitions playing inside her head: *Why hadn't Kenny fixed the damn doorbell the first six or seven times I asked him? Why hadn't I gotten up to investigate when I'd heard Bandit barking at the window? Why? Why? Why?*

She heard the sliding glass door open and turned to see Kenny walk outside onto the patio. Bandit waddled out behind him.

"Dishes are all done," he said, wiping his hands on his shirt.

"Thanks, baby."

He sat down beside her on the loveseat. "Feeling better?"

"Starting to," she said, taking another sip of wine.

Bandit padded down the patio stairs and took off like a furry groundhog after the pair of squirrels. One scampered over the fence and into a neighboring yard. The other scrambled up a tree. Bandit circled the base of it, sniffing in circles and whining.

"You sure you don't want me to call the newspaper and file a complaint?"

She shook her head. "I shouldn't have gotten so upset. It just…caught me by surprise."

"I'm afraid it's probably going to get worse before it gets better," he said. "I checked my voice mail. There were two messages from reporters. One from some lady at Channel Two and the other from a newspaper in Pittsburgh."

"Delete them please."

He reached over and rubbed her leg. "Already done."

Bandit suddenly started barking and charged the split-rail fence at the side of the yard.

Sarah tensed.

And quickly exhaled when it became apparent that it was happy barking and their next-door neighbor was the reason.

"Evening, folks, didn't mean to startle you," Paul Blauner said. He leaned over the fence to pet a gleeful Bandit. "Easy now. That's a good boy." He laughed delightedly, and after the day they'd had, it was a wonderful sound to hear.

"I think he smells the surprise I have for him," Paul said, scratching behind the dog's ears. "Don't you, boy?"

"You spoil him," Kenny said, smiling.

"I've told you kids before: no such thing as spoiling a good dog." He pulled something wrapped in a greasy paper towel out of his pants pocket. "Ready, boy?"

He unfolded the paper towel and tossed a steak bone high into the air. It landed in the middle of the yard. Bandit spun around on stubby legs and darted forward, snatching the bone out of the grass. He started padding toward the house, and then changed his mind, swinging in a wide circle and laying down in the shade of the big oak tree in which he had chased the squirrel earlier.

"He picked a good spot," Paul said, looking up at his neighbors. "He can scare the rabbits away from your vegetables over there."

Sarah winced at the mention of her garden. Kenny sensed her discomfort and swooped in. "You know as well as I do, Bandit couldn't catch one of those rabbits in his wildest dreams."

"Never say never," Paul said flatly. He checked his wristwatch and made a face. "I'm headed back to my den, folks. Almost time for *60 Minutes*."

"Thanks for the treat," Kenny said.

"My pleasure," Paul called over his shoulder and disappeared into the house.

"You okay?" Kenny asked, glancing at his wife.

Sarah rested her head on his shoulder. "I'm fine."

"You hardly said a word."

"I know. I guess I'm still feeling a little…fragile. And drunk." She surprised him by giggling. "And horny."

"Then, by all means, please keep drinking," he said, and they both cracked up laughing.

Out in the yard, Bandit rolled over onto his back, steadying the bone in his mouth with two chubby paws.

"I didn't like it when he mentioned the garden," she said suddenly.

Kenny nodded, his smile fading.

"It felt…weird after finding the footsteps. Just odd timing."

"I could tell," Kenny said.

"It made me think…" She hesitated.

"What?"

"I feel bad saying this but—even before we found the footprints—I'd been starting to feel so paranoid about everything. And everyone."

"You're talking about Paul?" he asked, surprised.

"I'm talking about a lot of people," Sarah said thoughtfully. "Including Paul."

"He's a sweet old man, honey. You know that."

She nodded. "I do know that. I do. It's just…"

"Go on," he said, encouraging her.

"I saw something last night. While you were playing poker." She glanced at the back of Paul's house and lowered her voice. "I wasn't spying on him, I swear. I was looking for dirty dishes in Natalie's room and I happened to peek out the window. You know how it looks down on Paul's driveway?"

Kenny nodded.

"The Cadillac was parked in the garage, but I could see the trunk was open and Paul was loading something inside. Something about the size and shape of a body."

Kenny jerked his head up. "Honey—"

Sarah held up a hand. "You got me started on this, let me finish and then you can tell me I'm crazy."

"I'm not going to—"

"I know it was probably just my imagination. You don't even have to say that. It could have been an old rug he was hauling away. Or a bundle of old clothes. Or pretty much anything else. But I'm telling you what I saw."

She got to her feet and reached out for Kenny's hand. "And now I'm done talking about it for tonight. I think it's time we go inside and see if all this wine has made me more adventurous."

Kenny shot to his feet and took his wife's hand, the troubling thoughts vanishing from his head.

They walked inside holding hands and locked the patio door behind them. By the time they reached the family room, they were kissing. By the time they stumbled into the foyer, Kenny's shirt was lying on the hardwood floor and Sarah's blouse was untucked and unbuttoned.

Sarah pulled her mouth away from his just long enough to make sure the deadbolt on the front door was locked—and that's when she saw the unmarked sedan parked across the street at Tom Carpenter's house.

"Look," she said, twisting away from her husband and pointing out one of the narrow, decorative windows that bookended the door. Her voice was husky and breathless.

Eager to continue the journey upstairs, Kenny peered out the window.

Detectives Jenkins and Giambanco stood on their neighbor's front porch. The door swung open and Tom Carpenter stepped back to allow the two detectives to enter the house. He closed the door behind them.

Sarah looked at her husband. Kenny looked at his wife.

The mood was broken.

SARAH ROLLED OVER and glanced at the alarm clock: 1:14 a.m. Twenty-seven minutes since the last time she'd checked. She looked at her sleeping husband beside her and once again considered waking him.

When Sarah and Kenny had first been married, more than twenty long years ago, they would often take turns waking each other in the middle of the night if one of them were having trouble sleeping. They'd turn on the television and watch a movie or they'd cuddle in the dark and talk about their worries, hopes, and dreams...until either they fell asleep in each other's arms or the morning sun kissed the bedroom window.

But things were different now. They were older and wiser (not to mention, supposedly braver). Besides, Kenny had school in the morning and he hadn't been sleeping well himself thanks to everything that'd happened recently.

Sarah considered turning on the bedside lamp so she could read her book, but she worried the light would disturb him, so instead she slid her cellphone off the end table and propped herself up with a couple of pillows.

She surfed Facebook for a while—the glow of the screen highlighting the dark circles beneath her eyes—and caught up on the lives of family and friends. But by the time she'd stumbled upon the video of the woman on her front porch for the fourth or fifth time, she decided enough was enough and clicked onto Instagram. It wasn't much better over there, and after a few minutes, she gave up.

She was trying to decide whether to play online Scrabble or solitaire when she noticed the camera-shaped icon for their home security system in the bottom row of the screen.

She tapped on it.

A prompt asked for a password.

She typed **n-a-t-b-u-g**—and she was in.

She avoided the button for ARCHIVED FOOTAGE—she'd seen the video from last Thursday enough times to last her a lifetime—and instead clicked on LIVE FEED.

A grainy night-vision image of the front porch flashed onscreen. The time code in the upper right-hand corner read: 1:19 a.m.

She watched as it switched over to 1:20 a.m.

And then a dark figure walked onto the porch.

Her heart trip-hammered.

The man was wearing dark pants and a dark sweatshirt. The hood was pulled tight, obscuring his face. His boots left a staggered track of muddy footprints across the porch, and Sarah realized where the man had just come from—the back yard.

She shuddered.

The man reached out and tried the doorknob, but it was locked. He crept over to the nearest window and tried to open it.

Sarah suddenly felt like a character from one of those old-fashioned mystery movies she liked to watch—usually it was the beautiful heroine who'd been slipped some kind of mysterious potion that caused total paralysis while keeping the poor woman conscious and aware of her surroundings. She wanted to yell for Kenny, to turn and wake him, but she couldn't do either. She was frozen.

The man on the front porch pulled a long, shiny blade from underneath his sweatshirt and wedged it between the window frame and the latch.

Sarah opened her mouth to cry out but could only manage a terrified moaning. She lifted her elbow and jabbed her husband's side. But it wasn't hard enough. He didn't stir.

The man jimmied the knife up and down in the narrow gap next to the window latch, and then he stopped and used both hands to push up—and the window started to slide open.

The sight of the window slowly inching upward finally broke Sarah free of her invisible shackles. She turned and shook her husband as hard as she could—and realized with mounting terror that he wasn't there.

The dark shape next to her in bed was nothing more than a pile of pillows arranged underneath a blanket. She was all alone.

The man on the porch bent down and swung one leg over the windowsill. Right before he pulled in his other leg and disappeared into the darkness of the downstairs living room, the man glanced over his shoulder to check out the street—and his hood fell away from his face.

Sarah gasped.

The man on the porch was Kenny.

He grinned menacingly at the empty street and was gone.

Sarah started to scream then—and as she awakened in a tangle of sweat-soaked blankets and sheets, her hand stuffed over her mouth, her husband beside her finally woke up.

MONDAY

SARAH WIPED beads of sweat from her face with a clean towel.

"I swear that bitch is the devil," Angie said, chugging from a bottle of water.

Sarah laughed and tossed the towel into the hamper beneath the EXIT sign.

"She's right," their friend Zoey said, still trying to catch her breath. "It's supposed to be an intermediate-level spin class. Not a goddam Olympic training session."

The three women walked outside into the parking lot.

"Tell me why we come to the gym again," Sarah said.

Zoey gave her a look. "So we look good in our new clothes, of course."

"And out of them," Angie added in typical Angie fashion.

Sarah laughed. "I'm stopping at Target on the way home if anyone wants to join."

"I will," Zoey said. "I want to hear all about this handsome number one suspect who lives right across the street from you."

"Number one suspect?" Sarah said. "I'm not sure what you're talking about."

"Oh, come on," Zoey said. "Beth told me all about him. Tall, dark, and handsome. The cops are all over him. You two have been holding out on me."

"I actually barely know him. None of us do. Tell her, Angie."

"She's right," Angie said. "The guy's a loner. Very quiet and mysterious. It's kinda sexy if you ask me. Most guys slobber all over you if you so much as smile at them. Tom Carpenter barely makes eye contact."

"Sounds yummy," Zoey said, licking her lips.

They reached their cars in the parking lot.

"I just remembered I have to drop off a notebook for Natalie at school," Sarah lied. "We'll have to do Target another day."

"Oh, darn," Zoey pouted.

All of a sudden, Sarah had the urge to slap her.

"See you girls next time," she said, getting into her car. "Give me a call later, Ang."

Angie gave her a wave and Sarah sped away.

* * *

SARAH TURNED THE corner and saw the detectives' car parked at the curb in front of the house. Her hands immediately broke out in a clammy sweat and for a moment she considered driving right on past. *But how would that look?* she thought, already knowing the answer.

Instead, she swung into the driveway and turned off the engine. By the time she opened the door and got out, Detectives Jenkins and Giambanco were waiting for her in the front yard.

"Good morning, Mrs. Tucker," Detective Jenkins said.

"I'm sorry, my husband's not here," Sarah said. "He has school today." *Of course, they would know that,* she thought and the realization made her heart beat even faster.

"That's fine. We came to speak with you today."

"Oh? About what?"

"Just a few questions. Would it be okay if we went inside?"

"The house is a mess," Sarah said, thinking fast. She didn't know what they wanted, but she figured the whole thing would probably go a lot faster if they didn't go inside and sit down.

"The front porch it is then," Detective Jenkins said. She extended her arm: *after you.*

Sarah and Detective Jenkins sat in hand-painted wooden chairs positioned at opposite ends of a small metal table. Detective Giambanco sat down on the stoop and turned to the side so he was facing them.

"So how can I help you?" Sarah asked once they were all settled.

Detective Jenkins flipped open her notepad. "Your husband is close friends with Ian Warrick and Trey Whiteford, is that right?"

"We're both close to Ian and Trey, and their families. My husband has known the two of them since high school."

"And both men currently live in the neighborhood?"

"Yes." Pointing. "Ian's on Patterson and Trey's on Lake Avenue."

"All the families socialize with each other?"

Sarah shrugged. "I mean we don't go on vacations together or anything like that, but sure. We get together for cookouts or to watch football. That sort of thing."

"Were you close to Trey Whiteford's ex-wife?" Detective Giambanco asked.

"Melody?" Sarah said, surprised by the question.

He glanced at his own notepad, which Sarah hadn't noticed before now. "Melody Hathaway."

"We were very close before the divorce. Not so much anymore, but we still text occasionally and exchange Christmas cards. I know she's remarried and living somewhere near Boston."

"Trey and Melody were together for a little over four years," Detective Giambanco said. "Do you recall the reason for their split?"

"I don't think there was any single reason for it. They just seemed to drift apart."

"No third party involved?"

Sarah's eyes narrowed. "No, nothing like that."

"Ever hear any stories or rumors about Trey being abusive in any manner?"

Sarah shook her head angrily. "That's the most ridiculous thing I've ever heard."

"So that's a 'no'?" Detective Jenkins said.

"Yes," Sarah said. "I mean, right, that's a big 'no.'"

"Were you aware of Ian Warrick's past financial troubles?" Detective Jenkins asked.

Sarah took a deep breath. "Ian never tried to hide it. He got in trouble with credit cards and student loans and had to declare bankruptcy. He was twenty-four, detective."

"I understand your husband had some trouble of his own during his younger days," Detective Giambanco said.

"What are you talking about?" Sarah asked, a chill tickling her spine.

He consulted his notes. "Spent ten days in Aberdeen Correctional for aggravated assault and destruction of property. Two stints in rehab. First one in 1997, and then again in 1999."

Sarah had finally had enough. "My husband hasn't had a drink in twenty years, Detective," she said, getting to her feet. "I don't know why you're digging up all this dirt about Ken and his friends instead of trying to catch whoever took that woman, but I'm finished with this conversation. If you have any further questions, you can contact my husband."

And with that she walked into the house, closed the door, and locked it behind her.

~~~

"STILL CAN'T BELIEVE you slammed the door in their faces," Kenny said, grinning.

"I wouldn't say I slammed it exactly."

He sat down next to Sarah on the sofa, balancing a plate of cheese and crackers on his lap. "I'm proud of you, honey. Thanks for sticking up for me."

"They had no business asking those kind of questions. What was the point? Obviously, you guys had nothing to do with that woman's disappearance."

Kenny picked up the remote and switched the channel to Monday Night Football. "I guess it's just part of the investigation. Checking into everyone's backgrounds."

"But why ask *me* about it? Why not talk to you guys directly?"

He shrugged. "Dunno."

"They knew you wouldn't be home." She shuddered. "The whole thing felt so…icky."

"Well, you did good. I doubt they're going to bother you anymore."

Sarah slumped back into the sofa cushions. She looked very small next to her husband. "I was really scared, Kenny. I was afraid one of them was going to bring up... *her*."

Kenny leaned forward and slid the snack plate onto the coffee table. He muted the television and turned to his wife. "I'm sorry, baby. I should have thought of that."

"I don't think I could've handled it if they had." She was on the verge of tears.

Kenny took her hand in his. "Listen to me. There's no way they could know about any of that. It happened a long time ago. It happened once. And it will never happen again. You know that, right?"

Sarah didn't say anything. Just nodded her head.

"I love you, Sarah Lynn Tucker. Only you."

A single tear trickled down her cheek. "I love you too. So much."

He wiped away the tear with his finger. "Just remember: We did nothing wrong. We didn't hear the woman ring the stupid doorbell or we would have—"

"That's what I just told the guy outside," Natalie said, walking into the family room. Neither of them had heard her in the foyer. She plopped down in the recliner and propped her feet up.

"What guy?" Sarah asked, immediately on alert.

"I don't know. Just some guy."

"What do you mean, 'just some guy'? What were you doing outside alone after dark? Didn't we tell you—"

"Whoa, chill out," Natalie said, flashing her mother a dirty look. "Dad told me to put my bike in the garage, so that's what I did."

Sarah glared at her husband. First, the horrible nightmare, then the surprise visit from the detectives, and now this.

"Sorry," he said. "I wasn't thinking."

She turned to her daughter. "Was it a reporter?"

"How am I supposed to know? He didn't have a nametag on saying 'I'm a reporter,' if that's what you're asking."

"Don't be a smart ass, Natalie."

"I'm not being a smart ass. You're the one giving me grief. All I did was put my bike away and some guy drove up and asked if I was Natalie Tucker and a couple other questions."

"Jesus," Sarah said, feeling like she might be sick.

Kenny got up from the sofa and headed into the kitchen.

"Where are you going?" she asked.

"To call the police."

THE POLICE OFFICER Kenny spoke with hadn't been able to reach Detective Jenkins, but Detective Giambanco called back fifteen minutes later.

Kenny explained what had happened and the detective asked him to put Natalie on speakerphone. Once he introduced himself, Detective Giambanco guided the teenager step-by-step through her story, encouraging her to remember important details—*What did the man look like?* (Dark hair, big nose, muscular arms); *What kind of car was he driving?* (I think it was a red Mustang, but it could have been a black Corvette); *Anything else you can remember?* (The car smelled like cigarette smoke and there was a big dent on the driver's side door)—without ever once pressuring her.

Although he'd been careful not to mention it later to Sarah, Kenny had been very impressed with the detective's soft touch and professionalism.

After having a fifteen-minute heart-to-heart sitting on the floor in Natalie's bedroom—(Sarah: "I'm sorry I yelled at you, honey; I was scared and worried." Natalie: "I'm sorry I acted like such a smart ass; I was being defensive.")—Natalie was now sound asleep and Sarah was upstairs getting ready for bed.

Kenny stood at the top of the driveway, eyes scanning the deepening gloom. Nothing moved, not even a stray cat or dog on the prowl. There were no strange cars cruising the road with dimmed headlights. No shadowy figures lurking behind trees or the unlit corners of houses. Most of the homes on the street were dark. He glanced at Tom Carpenter's house and saw the flickering glow of a television screen in a second-floor window. Kenny pictured Tom lying under the blankets alone watching a movie in his upstairs bedroom, and the thought made him feel sad and even a little lonely.

Finally, he grabbed the trashcan by the handle and rolled it down the driveway to the curb, the slap of his bare feet surprisingly loud in the silence. The crisp autumn air felt good on his face, like a wake-up kiss on a lazy Sunday morning. Stars blanketed the night sky above. Hundreds of them like sparkling diamonds strewn across velvet. It was a beautiful, calming sight.

So why, Kenny thought, as he walked back to the garage, *was he convinced that the worst was yet to come?*

⁓

THE MAN WAITED for the automatic garage door to close and then he climbed down the tree and dropped to the ground. He tightened the hood over his head and felt for the knife in his waistband. Then he melted into the shadows.

TUESDAY

UESDAY WAS a welcome return to normalcy for the Tucker family.

Natalie aced two quizzes in school and was asked to the Halloween dance by the second cutest boy in the seventh grade (this according to best friend, Madison, who believed the woman from the video was an escaped alien).

Sarah reported no strange cars stopping at the house and no surprise visits from the detectives. She spent her day grocery shopping, standing in line at the pharmacy in Target, and cleaning the house from top to bottom. She only thought of the woman in the video approximately fifty times, which she claimed was a huge step in the right direction.

For Kenny, the school day passed in a blur of pre-exam review sessions, and for the first time in nearly twenty-four hours, not a single soul asked him about the video. He spoke with Sarah twice by phone during the day. Once at lunch and again right before practice, when it was decided that he would pick up Chinese carryout for dinner on his way home.

His stomach rumbled as he pulled away from The Orient at ten minutes past six, the smell of spicy Szechuan beef and shrimp lo mein filling the pick-up truck's interior.

Kenny struggled to drive the speed limit home and had to force himself not to ransack the brown paper bag sitting beside him for one of those clear little wax baggies full of crispy Chinese noodles. Those were his favorite.

By the time he spotted his house in the distance he was hungry enough to eat the brown paper bag itself. He swung into the driveway and saw Tom Carpenter getting out of his car across the street.

He waved but was pretty sure Tom didn't see him.

So he was doubly surprised when his neighbor called out his name and strolled over to talk.

"How you doing, Ken?" he said.

Kenny smiled nervously and shook Tom's hand. "Doing okay. How about you?"

Tom glanced at the ground. "Not so good, actually. Someone killed my cat Sunday night."

"What?" Kenny asked, not sure he'd heard correctly.

"I went to an early movie and when I got home I found her in the back yard. Someone had…cut her open."

"Jesus Christ. Why would anyone do that?"

"That's what I asked the detectives. They'd left their cards when they'd interviewed me about the woman in your video and asked me to call if I noticed anything suspicious."

"What did they say?" Kenny asked.

"Not much. They poked around the back yard for a little while and put Ginger in a plastic bag for evidence. I'm supposed to get her back so I can give her a proper burial, but they didn't say when."

Kenny shook his head. "Damn. I'm sorry, Tom."

"You didn't see anything out of the ordinary this weekend, did you?"

"Nothing," Kenny said, and then added: "Actually, *everything* feels out of the ordinary since the video."

Tom nodded. "I know what you mean. You should see the nasty looks I'm getting from the neighbors."

Kenny felt his face flush with guilt. "Well, I better get dinner inside before Sarah and Nat come looking for me."

"Sure thing," Tom said, turning to leave. "Tell them I said hello."

"Will do. I'm sorry again about Ginger."

"Me too," Tom said. "Me too."

Kenny started for the garage, and then stopped and turned around. "Hey, Tom."

Tom stopped and looked back at him.

"When the detectives came to the house the other day, they asked if we knew of any single people living in the neighborhood. I guess they wanted to know who could've possibly had a guest over in the middle of the night. We told them you and Paul."

Tom's eyes widened with surprise.

"But we also assured them neither you nor Paul could've had anything to do with that woman. We told them you were a great guy...just a little on the quiet side."

Tom remained silent for a moment. When he spoke again, his voice sounded even more dejected.

"Thanks for telling me, Ken. I appreciate it. I kind of figured it was something like that with all the dirty looks."

"I'm really sorry. People are idiots."

"Yes, they are," he said, nodding and walking away. "Yes, they are."

~~~

KENNY BELCHED AND tasted spicy Szechuan in the back of his throat. He spit out the window and was glad Sarah wasn't there to scold him.

He turned onto David's street and checked the rearview mirror to make sure the power-washer he'd loaded in the back of the pick-up hadn't shifted. That was the last thing he needed to do: damage his friend's property.

Kenny had known David Blessing since his freshman year in high school. He was a good guy and a lot of fun, despite being the most uptight personality in their circle, but he was also something else—a first-class cheapskate. David could pinch a penny with the best of them, and he was openly proud of that fact. Kenny and the others always joked that David should've been an accountant instead of an insurance salesman.

Kenny slowed and coasted to a stop at the curb in front of David's sprawling rancher. The house and lawn were immaculate. Not a single smudge on a single window. The manicured grass looked like it belonged on a golf course. Kenny didn't know how his friend did it. If he and Sarah had three young kids, like David and Jane, their lawn would probably look like a playground.

He climbed out of the truck and started loosening the straps holding the power-washer in place when he heard David's angry voice.

"Son of a bitch!"

Kenny dropped the strap and hurried toward the open garage. What he saw there made him hesitate and slowly ease behind David's SUV, which was parked at the head of the driveway.

"Where the fuck did I put it?" David fumed, flinging a cardboard box across the garage. He stormed over and kicked the box and it broke apart, spilling manila file folders and loose sheets of paper everywhere. "Fuck!" Red faced and breathing heavy, he stomped across the garage and picked up another box and started rifling through its contents.

Kenny stood there frozen. In all the years he had known David, he'd never once seen his friend lose his temper. Not like this. Sure, he got upset from time to time, usually when his father was driving him crazy at the office or the guys were picking on him too much, but it usually resulted in a half-hearted, whiny request to back off or an unintentionally humorous insult leftover from their teenaged days. "Suck my dick, you pecker-heads," was a David Blessing specialty.

But this was something altogether different.

This was raw and visceral and frightening.

Kenny thought about sneaking to his truck and tapping the horn, so David would think he'd just pulled up. But he didn't think he could look his friend in the eye and hide what he'd just witnessed. He decided returning the power-washer could wait for another day and backpedaled his way down the driveway. He carefully opened the truck door and slipped inside. He started the engine, cringing at the loud rumble, and quickly sped away.

"I'M TELLING YOU, you had to be there," Kenny said, rinsing his toothbrush. "It was bizarre."

Sarah finished brushing her hair in the mirror. "Now you sound like me talking about Paul."

Kenny looked at his wife. She had a point. "It was just so…upsetting. I didn't know what to do. I wish I had never been there to see it."

Sarah walked out of the bathroom and crawled into bed. "If it's bothering you that much, call him up and ask him."

"Hell no. That's the last thing I want to do is talk about it."

"Maybe he needs your help, Kenny. You ever think about that?"

He shook his head. "I guess not."

"I'm proud of you for being so honest with Tom Carpenter. I know it couldn't have been easy. Maybe David needs the same thing: someone to talk to."

"That was different. I had to tell Tom the truth. If you'd seen his face and heard his voice. It was the right thing to do."

"I never told you but I saw him at Barnes and Noble yesterday when I ran in to return Natalie's book. He was ten feet away from me. Instead of saying hello, I ducked into the magazine aisle and snuck away. I felt like such a coward."

"The poor guy's turning into a pariah."

"Seriously. A couple days ago, Angie was all about how sexy she thought Tom was. Today, she's convinced he's a serial killer."

Kenny slid under the covers. "That's Frank talking."

"I don't know," Sarah said. "Her and Frank don't agree on much."

Kenny looked at his wife. "Really? Tom…sexy?"

Sarah shrugged. "You know Angie."

"Do *you* think he's sexy?"

Sarah smiled. "Kenny Tucker, are you jealous?"

"Of course not," he said, shaking his head. "Just curious is all."

Sarah cuddled closer. She was enjoying this. "Well, as a matter of fact, I do not think Tom Carpenter is sexy." She traced a finger up and down her husband's arm. "But you, mister, you're an entirely different story."

Kenny leaned over and turned off the bedside lamp.

WEDNESDAY

THE LAST thing Sarah wanted to do this morning was go to the gym. But she'd promised Angie she'd be there, so that was that.

She drove slowly down the street, thinking about making love with Kenny the night before. It had surprised her how good it had been. No, that wasn't right. It hadn't merely been good, it'd been amazing. She smiled and hit the button to lower her window.

At that moment, Paul Blauner drove past, heading in the opposite direction. He lifted a liver spotted hand and waved.

Sarah reached out the window and gave him an enthusiastic wave back and tooted the horn. She still felt bad about what she'd told Kenny. Paul was the sweetest old man she'd ever known. He was practically part of the family after all these years. She would have to make it up to him somehow.

As she approached the four-way intersection ahead, Sarah noticed a dark green car parked along the left side of the road in the shade of one of Rhonda Marshall's big oak trees.

She slowed down and studied the vehicle.

There were several deep scratches on the driver's side door panel and the rear left tire was missing a hubcap. The windows were tinted, but she could just make out the dark shape of someone slouched down in the driver's seat. *Could it be a cop?* she wondered, turning on her blinker and taking a right at the stop sign. After the appearance of the mysterious woman and what happened to Tom Carpenter's poor cat, she wouldn't have been at all surprised to learn that there were undercover officers patrolling the neighborhood. Just thinking about it made her feel safer.

But what if it wasn't a cop? Then who? A reporter? It was certainly possible. They were still leaving messages on Kenny's cellphone and one had stopped by the house the day before yesterday.

What if it wasn't a cop or *a reporter?* her mind teased. *What if it was* him?

Sarah picked up her cellphone to call Kenny at school but hesitated. Last night had been like a dream and she didn't want anything to burst the happy, sleepy bubble she felt enveloped within.

She put down the phone.

It could wait.

"IT'S LIKE WALKING a tortoise."

"Hush," Sarah said, swatting her husband on the shoulder. "He'll hear you."

Kenny glanced at his wife and then down at Bandit. "Umm, he's a dog."

"And he's sensitive," she said, putting out her hand. "Just give it to me."

He handed over the leash.

It had been Sarah's idea to take a walk after dinner. The temperature had dropped into the upper fifties the past few days and the leaves were beginning to turn. Vibrant colors blanketed the neighborhood and the scent of wood smoke hung thick in the air. After an unnaturally long and hot summer, it was finally beginning to feel like autumn.

"He's not used to walking on a leash," she said. "That's why he's walking so slow."

"Oh, okay. I thought it had something to do with the fact that his legs are three inches long."

Sarah giggled.

"Well, well, well," Kenny said, spotting his friend, Trey, up ahead. He was down on his hands and knees, spreading mulch around the handful of bushes that bordered his front porch. A stack of large mulch bags waited behind him. "Will miracles never cease?"

Trey looked up and grimaced. His face was streaked with dirt. "Shut it, Kenny."

"Hey there, Trey," Sarah said.

"Hey there, Sarah."

"Carly home?"

"Inside helping Pete with his math homework."

She handed Kenny the leash and cut across the lawn. "I need to ask her about Jane's birthday lunch. Back in a flash."

Trey got to his feet and wiped his hands on his jeans. Gave Bandit a pat on the head. "Ready for patrol tonight?"

"Not really. Are you?"

Trey shrugged. "Could be fun."

"Probably not."

Trey nodded. "Probably not."

Behind them, a police cruiser drove slowly by. Kenny lifted his hand and waved. The driver just looked at him and kept going.

"And there goes our friendly neighborhood police officer," Trey said, watching the car until it turned the corner.

"What a dick."

"Second time he's driven past in the last thirty minutes."

"I guess we're supposed to feel safe now."

"A detective stopped by my office today."

Kenny looked at his friend in surprise. "Are you serious?"

Nodding. "Detective Jenkins. She caught up with me in the parking lot as I was leaving." He gave Kenny a questioning look. "Figured you sent her my way."

"I would never," Kenny said, shaking his head emphatically. "She stopped by the house two days ago when I wasn't home. Asked Sarah a couple questions about you and Ian. Kind of freaked her out."

"You didn't think I would want to know about something like that?"

Kenny felt the heat rush to his face. "I honestly didn't think anything would come of it. I'm sorry. You're right. I should've called you right away."

"You tell Ian?"

A reluctant nod. "Only because he stopped by the house later that evening. But even then, Sarah had to remind me."

Trey stared at Kenny, lips pressed tightly together, eyes narrowed. The streaks of dirt on his cheeks and forehead looked like warpaint.

For a fleeting moment, Kenny was certain that his longtime friend was about to explode in anger—but then the moment passed and Trey was suddenly grinning at him.

"I'm just yanking your chain, buddy. It's all good. Caught me by surprise is all."

"That was my fault." He sighed. "I should've warned you. I'm sorry."

"Don't sweat it," Trey said, picking up another bag of mulch. "Just do me a favor, will you?"

"Sure thing."

"I'd hate for it to get back to Carly and her start worrying about nothing. You know how she is."

Kenny nodded. "Not a problem. I'll mention it to Sarah." And then eager to change the subject: "Hey, you hear from David lately?"

"Not since poker. I've been swamped at the office."

"Have you noticed anything…unusual about him lately?"

"Unusual how?"

"I don't know. Distracted maybe? Impatient? Irritable?"

"Nothing like that," Trey said, shaking his head. "Why you ask?"

"I ran into him the other day. He wasn't himself."

"Probably work. I've never met anyone who hates his job as much as—"

"Told you I'd be quick," Sarah said, coming out the door. She took the leash back from her husband and looked at Trey. "Carly told me to tell you that if you don't finish mulching you can't go out and play with the boys tonight."

Trey smiled. "If you don't see me later, Kenny, you'll know why."

"Don't you dare. You better be there."

Trey tore open the bag of mulch, grunting with the effort. "No worries. I think Ian would disown me if I no-showed."

Bandit started tugging on his leash.

"Gotta go," Kenny said. "The tortoise grows impatient."

TREY GROANED. "I feel like a moron."

"You look like a moron," David said.

"Look who's talking," Craig said. "You look like an anorexic seal."

It was nine o'clock and the five of them were standing in a circle in Ian's front yard. They were all dressed in dark clothing. Sweatpants and sweatshirts for Kenny and Trey. Jeans and sweaters for Craig and Ian. For some reason, David had opted for black skin-tight running pants and an equally snug long-sleeve Under Armour cold-gear shirt. He did indeed resemble an anorexic seal.

"Whose idea was it to dress like cat burglars?" Craig asked. "We're supposed to be the good guys."

"We need to blend in with our surroundings in order to properly observe," Ian said. He held up a small cylinder. "Anyone need pepper spray?"

Kenny looked around at his friends and started laughing.

"What's so funny?" Trey asked.

"I was just thinking about what our wives would say if they could see us right now. We'd never hear the end of it."

"Jane saw me leave the house," David said. "She said I looked adorable."

"God bless that woman," Craig snorted.

"We're wasting time," Ian said, checking his wristwatch. "I have nine-oh-four. Everyone synchronize their watches."

Kenny held up his arm. "I'm not wearing a watch."

"Neither am I," David said.

Trey and Craig showed him their bare wrists.

"Jesus," Ian said. "Do you at least have your phones?"

"Got that," Craig said, smiling. The others held up their cellphones.

"I say we split up into two groups," Ian continued. "One group heads north and cuts back on Regal. The other group heads south and circles around when they hit Sycamore." He looked at the other men. "What do you think?"

Kenny shrugged. "Sounds good to me."

"What are the groups?" Trey asked.

"How about Kenny and I head north?" David said. "The three of you go south."

"Fine with me," Craig agreed.

"That okay with you, Kenny?" David asked.

"Sure," Kenny said, thinking about the bizarre incident he'd witnessed in David's garage. His mind immediately started working: *Why was David so anxious to be partnered with him? Craig was his closest friend; why not pick him? And why just the two of them?*

"Okay, let's get moving," Ian said, taking charge again. "Rendezvous back here at ten o'clock. We'll compare notes, regroup, and head out on another mission."

Craig looked at Kenny. "Did he just say 'another mission'?"

"'Fraid so."

"Don't even bother trying to reason with him," David said, starting to walk up the street. "He's lost in his own little fantasy world."

"Ten sharp," Ian said, ignoring him. "Don't be late."

Kenny said goodbye to the others and hurried to catch up with David. "This was actually your bright idea, you know?" he said when he reached his friend's side.

David nodded. "I thought it would be interesting. When else are we going to have a chance to do something like this?"

"I guess."

"And who knows, maybe we'll find something."

"Like what?"

"Hard to say. But could you imagine if we found the woman from the video and rescued her?"

Kenny took a deep breath. "I have a feeling we're never going to see that woman again. No one is."

"Maybe not, but we'd be heroes if we found her or captured the guy who made her disappear." David stopped at the crossroad. "Where did Sarah see that green car this morning?"

"In front of Bill Marshall's house."

"Then what are we waiting for?" David said, and started walking again. "Let's go."

IT WAS IAN'S idea, of course, to have one person walk down the middle of the road while the other two patrolled the sidewalks on the opposite sides of the street. "This way we cover more ground," he said. "And no one will be able to slip past us."

Craig agreed to the plan—and took his place on the sidewalk at the right side of the road—just so he didn't have to listen to Ian's mouth the rest of the night. Trey—who ended up on the left side—would've waited all night for the Great Pumpkin in the middle of a desolate, tick-infested field of sticker-bushes if it meant getting further away from Ian (who, of course, was now strolling down the center of Juniper Lane, most likely imagining he was walking point in the danger-filled jungles of Viet Nam).

"All clear," he whispered, scanning the dark road ahead.

"All clear," Trey answered a few seconds later.

And finally Craig: "Clear."

They walked the next several minutes in silence.

Someone in a nearby house opened a door and quickly closed it again, letting out the family pet for his or her nightly business.

A car cruised slowly down the street, and Ian stepped aside to let it pass, straining to get a glimpse of the driver, making a mental note of the car's model and year.

A snatch of music drifted on the autumn air and was gone before any of the men could identify the tune.

They marched around the long, winding bend that marked the end of Juniper, and as the old-fashioned streetlight on the corner of Sycamore came into view, Craig let out a high-pitched scream.

The other men came running, Ian reaching his side first. "What's wrong?" he asked, eyes wide. A breathless Trey arrived a moment later. "What happened? Are you okay?"

Craig looked down at the ground and kicked a tuft of grass. "I, uhhh, think it was a rabbit."

"A rabbit?" Ian asked, incredulous.

"It jumped out of the bush right in front of me. Scared me."

"Christ," Trey said. "I think I pissed my pants."

Ian scowled. "Everyone back to their positions." He glanced at his watch. "We have twenty minutes before we circle back and meet the others."

"A fucking rabbit," Trey said, walking away.

Ian took his place in the center of the street again. Sycamore was one of two original roadways that bisected the Broadview development, existing long before the neighborhood expanded around it. It was wider than the newer streets by almost fifteen feet and surrounded by majestic, towering oak trees. Once the three men left the streetlight behind, it felt as if they were walking into the mouth of a dark cavernous tunnel.

Ian scanned from left to right and back again, but it was no use: it was impossible to see more than ten or so yards in front of him. The moon slipped behind a cluster of clouds and the night grew dead quiet.

"All clear," he said, voice cracking.

Silence greeted him.

"All clear," he said again, louder this time.

No response.

"This isn't funny, guys."

Nothing.

Ian suddenly swerved to the right side of the roadway. "Trey? Stop fucking around."

But Trey wasn't there.

Scared now, he jogged to the opposite side of the road. "Craig! Where are you?"

The sidewalk was empty. Craig was nowhere in sight.

"Trey! Craig!"

Somewhere in the distance a dog howled and the silver moon floated out from behind the clouds.

Ian started running.

"YOU OKAY?" DAVID asked.

"I'm fine," Kenny said. "A little banged up."

They were working their way up Regal, headed back to Ian's house. So far, the night had been a total bust. The only action they'd seen was when a kid on a bike nearly gave David a heart attack and not long after Kenny tripped over an uneven section of sidewalk and almost knocked himself unconscious. His head still ached from where he'd collided with the tree trunk.

"I guess maybe this wasn't a good idea after all," David said.

Kenny didn't say anything. He rubbed the bump on his forehead and checked his fingers to see if it was bleeding. It was too dark to tell.

"I keep thinking about something my father said at the office today."

"What's that?" Kenny asked, suddenly interested. David's father was a sharp guy. And he knew his football. Kenny liked him a lot.

"He said that if the woman had escaped from someone in the neighborhood and the person had tracked her down later that night and recaptured her, then the person probably would've decided to kill her to make sure it didn't happen again or at least to erase any possible connection between the two of them."

"That's pretty fucking morbid."

"My dad loves true crime shows," David said. "Anyway, he went on to say that the person would eventually have to get rid of the body. Before it started to smell. He figured the guy would wait a few days until the heat died down, and then he'd move the body under the cover of darkness."

"Makes sense, I guess. But there are a lot of ways to get rid of a body. He could chop it up and carry it out of the house in five or six trips in a knapsack. And, hell, he could do that in broad daylight. Or he could bury it in the back yard or stuff it in the trunk of his car if he had a garage and no one would be the wiser."

"I never thought about that," David said. "I'll have to tell my father."

"Tell him it was your idea. He'll like that."

David smiled, and they walked in silence for a while.

"You think Tom Carpenter had anything to do with it?"

"Not a chance," Kenny said. "Tom's a stand-up guy. He's just an easy target right now."

David nodded. "I thought the same thing when we walked by his house earlier."

A car drove slowly past. The window was down and they could hear the radio playing. David checked it out. Kenny didn't even bother to look. He was done. The car's taillights faded to tiny red sparks in the distance and disappeared. David abruptly stopped walking.

"I know you were at my house yesterday."

Kenny's spine instantly turned to ice.

"And I know you were talking to Trey about me."

Kenny tried to say something, but his breath caught in the back of his throat.

"I'm sorry you had to see me like that."

Something about David's voice had changed. Kenny was suddenly afraid to look at him. He glanced around and realized where they were: the last undeveloped section of Broadview. There were houses a quarter mile ahead of them and houses a quarter mile behind them. Where they were standing, there was nothing but dark, empty lots. For one insane moment, he thought about running.

"I didn't mean to eavesdrop," Kenny finally said, his voice trembling. "I brought back your power-washer, but..."

"But what?"

"It...seemed like a bad time, so I decided to come back later."

David started walking again. "I lost Jane's anniversary present."

"What?" Kenny asked, confused.

"That's what I was looking for when you saw me. I bought her a necklace, a six thousand dollar necklace, as a surprise and hid it in the garage." He took a deep breath. "And then I couldn't remember where I hid the goddam thing."

"You're kidding me."

"I wish I was."

"So that's why you were freaking out? Because you couldn't find a necklace?"

"A six thousand dollar necklace."

Kenny whistled. "That *is* a lot of money...especially for you."

"Jane loved it, by the way."

"She better have," Kenny said, breathing easier now. "Where'd you end up finding it?"

"In a shoebox under my work bench. Right where I put it."

Kenny laughed and gave David a friendly shove. "Holy shit, man, you scared the hell outta me. I even told Sarah about it."

"It's pretty embarrassing," David said, sighing. "I was so damn mad at myself for misplacing it in the first place, and then I was even madder for losing my temper like that."

"How'd you know I saw you? Trey?"

He shook his head. "I heard your truck start up. Watched you drive away."

"I didn't know what else to—"

"Hey!" David said, pointing across the street at the far corner of an empty lot.

The dark figure emerging from the shadows obviously didn't see them standing there on the opposite side of the road. He moved stealthily, bent over in a crouch, heading in the direction of the nearest house.

"Son of a bitch," Kenny whispered.

"Let's get him," David said and took off running, with a surprised Kenny struggling to catch up.

They closed to within twenty yards before the man heard their heavy footfalls on the asphalt road. He jerked his head around, saw them coming, and immediately changed direction, swerving toward the side yard. He climbed over the fence and was gone.

"I'll cut him off," Kenny yelled, veering toward the opposite side of the house. David sprinted across the lawn and scrambled over the fence.

Kenny slowed down to squeeze between the corner of the garage and a row of shrubbery, and when he came out on the other side, he spotted the man's legs dangling from the top of the fence.

Kenny lunged and grabbed him by the ankles.

The man kicked wildly, landing a steel-toed boot to the side of Kenny's head.

Kenny's vision went blurry and, for the second time in less than an hour, he thought he might pass out.

"Cocksucker!" he shouted, grabbing hold of the man's leg and yanking him over the fence and onto the ground. And then he was on top of him, pinning the man's arms with his knees, and raining down punches on his face.

"Stop it!" the man screamed, twisting his head from side to side. "STOP!"

Kenny kept swinging—a right, a left, another right. The man on the ground squealed in pain.

"Stop!" David yelled, leaping down from the top of the fence. "It's Craig! It's Craig!" He dragged Kenny off of him and they collapsed in a heap to the ground.

Kenny lay there, bathed in sweat, trying to catch his breath. He shrugged David off of him. "What the fuck were you doing?" he yelled at Craig.

"Me?" Craig said, rubbing his jaw. "You almost killed me!"

"What were you doing sneaking around? Where are Ian and Trey?"

"We ditched Ian because he was acting like an asshole. And then we got separated. I don't know where the hell Trey is." Craig pushed himself up to his feet, wobbled unsteadily, and leaned against the fence to regain his balance. "Christ, Kenny, you were like a pit bull."

"I'm sorry," he said, eyes still wild. "I was scared."

"You were scared?" David said, starting to grin. "I'd hate to see you when you're mad."

The back porch light flashed on. The patio door slid open and an older woman with her hair up in curlers poked her head out and waved a spatula at them. "You kids get outta my yard or I'm calling the cops!"

The three men took off running, their laughter echoing in the hush of the autumn night.

KENNY PULLED INTO the driveway and turned off the engine. He had a bump the size of a golf ball on his forehead and his knuckles were swollen and bruised from punching his friend in the face—but he was grinning like a little kid. It had turned out to be a fun night, after all.

When they'd gotten back to Ian's house, Trey had been sitting on the front stoop waiting for them. He'd had his own story of misadventure to share—involving a pair of bloodthirsty poodles. When David called bullshit, Trey displayed his shredded sweatpants as evidence. Fifteen minutes later, Ian showed up, pissy as hell, accusing Trey and Craig of insubordination. He'd felt a little better when he found out Kenny had given Craig a fat lip and what was probably going to be a heckuva shiner under his left eye.

Kenny got out of the truck, glanced over at Tom Carpenter's house. All the windows were dark. He hit the automatic lock on his key fob and climbed the steps onto the front porch. He was about to insert his key into the lock when he saw the piece of paper sitting on top of the doormat. He bent down and picked it up. It was one of the DO YOU KNOW THIS WOMAN? flyers the police had distributed all over town and to the news media.

Kenny folded the flyer in half and stuffed it into his back pocket and went inside.

It wasn't until later, when he was lying in bed in the dark, that he wondered if the piece of paper might have been left there as a warning.

THURSDAY

KENNY WAS washing his hands after lunch in the faculty bathroom when Charlie Finnigan, the junior/senior Chemistry teacher, opened the door and called out, "Hey, Kenny, someone here to see you." He turned to leave, then hesitated. "I think she's a cop."

"Thanks, Charlie." Kenny quickly dried his hands and, with a sinking feeling in his stomach, went outside into the break room. Detective Jenkins was seated at a table in the corner waiting for him.

"Everything okay?" Kenny asked, sitting down across from her.

"That's a nasty bump," she said, touching her own forehead. "What happened?"

"I was horsing around with some friends. It was stupid really."

"You ought to be more careful. You're not a teenager anymore, Mr. Tucker."

"My wife tells me that all the time."

"Anyway, I'm sorry to bother you at school, but there's been a break in the case and, well, it involves you in a peripheral manner."

"Me?" Kenny asked, surprised. "What happened? Did you find her?"

The detective shook her head. "We haven't located the woman in the video, but we *have* identified who she is."

"That's great news, right?"

"I'm going to share some information with you and ask that you keep it confidential for the time being," she said, pulling out her notepad. "You can tell your wife, but no one else, please. We're not even releasing this information to the press yet."

Kenny nodded. "Of course."

"We received a phone call this morning from a man claiming to be the stepfather of the woman in the video. Detective Giambanco and I met with the man and were able to verify his claim."

"Okay."

"Her name is Katherine Morris, age twenty-eight."

"She looks younger on the video."

"A longtime resident of Baltimore, Maryland."

"That's only an hour-and-a-half away from here," Kenny said, instantly feeling foolish for stating the obvious.

"Her stepfather lives in Delta, Pennsylvania. He hasn't seen Miss Morris for several years."

"So he doesn't have any idea what happened to her? Or what she was doing in Hanover?"

"None at all, unfortunately."

"How is any of this connected to me?" Kenny asked.

"Well, that's where it gets interesting." The detective looked down at her notes again. "Do you remember a student of yours from several years ago named Randy Jefferson?"

Kenny thought about it for a moment. The name sounded familiar but he couldn't pull up a face or any other details from his memory pool.

"This would be before you started teaching at Harford Day School," the detective continued. "When you were at South Hills."

Kenny shook his head. "I'm sorry. The name rings a bell but that's about it."

"Are you sure, Mr. Tucker?"

"I think so," Kenny said. "I've taught hundreds of kids over the years."

Studying her notes again: "Randy Jefferson was a freshman at South Hills in 2013. He was in your third period English Composition class."

"If you say so," Kenny said, his unease growing.

"We checked the school records."

"Okay, you checked the records," he said, suddenly annoyed. "Do you mind getting to the point? I have a class in ten minutes."

"Randy's parents were divorced in 2010. The father was out of the picture, so it's doubtful you ever crossed paths with him."

Kenny waited for her to continue.

"His mother, Ramona Jefferson, however, met with you on several occasions at South Hills. The usual parent teacher conferences."

"Okay."

"She has very kind things to say about your teaching abilities, by the way."

"That's nice to hear."

"Ramona Jefferson has a younger sister." She paused for effect. "Her name is Katherine Morris."

Kenny felt like he'd been punched in the gut. "You're kidding me?"

"As with the stepfather, she hasn't spoken with Katherine in a number of years."

Kenny's mind was spinning.

"In light of this information, would you like to rethink your answer to my previous question?"

"Which question?" Kenny asked, confused.

Detective Jenkins stared at him. "Have you ever met Katherine Morris?"

"No," Kenny said, shaking his head. "I swear I've never met the woman."

"Quite a coincidence then that Katherine showed up on your front porch at three-thirty in the morning, wouldn't you say?"

"She showed up at my next-door neighbor's house first," Kenny said, knowing how pathetic he sounded but not caring. "That has to mean something."

The detective looked at him and didn't say a word.

The school bell rang.

"YOU SHOULD HAVE heard him. He was so appreciative," Sarah said, sitting down at the dinner table. Natalie was at a friend's house studying for a math test, so it was just the two of them. "You would have thought I'd brought over a turkey dinner with all the trimmings instead of a plate of chocolate chip cookies."

"Paul likes his sweets," Kenny said absently.

"He told me again about his wife's top-secret cinnamon raisin cookie recipe."

Kenny laughed. "How many times is that now? A dozen?"

"Oh, more," she said, joining in the laughter.

"You feel better?"

She nodded. "I do. I was foolish to think that sweet man was up to no good."

"Don't be so hard on yourself, honey. Things have been strange lately."

"Tell me about it," she said. "I feel like life's just now starting to get back to normal."

Kenny gave his wife a look. "Well, not quite yet."

"What does that mean?"

"Detective Jenkins stopped by school today."

"What?" Sarah looked stricken. "And you're just now telling me?"

"I just got home twenty minutes ago," Kenny said.

"You could have called. You *should* have called."

"You're right," he said. "I should have."

"What did she say?"

He told her.

⟡

KENNY SAT ALONE in the dark.

Thursday night football—a Cowboys/Giants dogfight—was midway through the fourth quarter on television, but he was barely paying attention.

Sarah was upstairs in bed, presumably asleep. Her reaction to the news had been even worse than he'd expected. At first, she'd been wary and questioning ("Then how can you be so sure you've never met her?"), but as Kenny delved deeper into the story, she'd grown angry and downright accusatory ("I knew something was off about this whole thing!").

A Budweiser commercial came on the TV. Kenny watched as an attractive young woman wearing a bright yellow bikini tossed a frosty bottle of Bud to an attractive young man with six-pack abs and a square chin.

If I were ever tempted to sneak a drink, it would be right now, he thought, lying back on the sofa. *What a shitshow!*

But he wasn't tempted.

Not even a little bit.

That was the point. He was a different man now. Thanks to Sarah.

Kenny hadn't had a drink in twenty years and almost seven months. The last time he'd gone to rehab—after his third car accident in as many months—had stuck for good. Between finally buying into the program and Sarah's unfailing belief and support, he'd come out on the other side and made it.

The first six months had been rough—they'd been *hell,* to be perfectly honest—but things had eventually gotten better. And better. To the point where the craving had actually dissipated and the only thing left in its place was the occasional back-of-the-brain flicker of memory of a different person and a different life.

The next few years after that had felt like a prolonged honeymoon. He'd gotten a job working at a hardware store in the mornings and went back to school and finished getting his teaching degree in the evenings. Sarah had worked at the hospital and made good money as a therapist. They'd rented an apartment not far from her parents, and filled it with the things that mattered most to them: books and movies and paintings. They'd grown tomatoes and peppers on the balcony and repainted the walls of their bedroom once a year like clockwork.

Then, he'd landed his first teaching job and full-time salary, and they'd made plans to move into a condo by the river.

Six months later, Kenny slipped.

But alcohol wasn't the culprit this time.

Instead, it was a substitute teacher named Scarlett Webster. Fresh out of college, she was everything Sarah wasn't: introverted, needy, and lost. And Kenny had fallen victim to the oldest story in the book: the brave knight riding in on his magnificent steed to rescue the poor, victimized waif.

He hadn't allowed the relationship to become sexual, but it hadn't really mattered. There were texts and secrets and rendezvous for coffee and evening walks in the park.

When Sarah found out, she'd been devastated.

Within a week, she'd emptied the apartment of her belongings and moved in with her parents. For a month after, she'd refused to even speak to Kenny, sending only the occasional angry text.

Kenny was adrift without her. All the old memories and desires came crashing down on him—along with a double barrel blast of guilt and self-loathing—but he never faltered and took a drink. Instead, he doubled up on his AA meetings and started seeing a therapist twice a week.

The first thing the therapist helped him to understand was why he had strayed. It hadn't been love. And it certainly hadn't been lust. As happens with a lot of addicts, he'd simply become too comfortable in his new life, too happy and content, and something inside of his brain had gotten scared and panicked—and attempted to sabotage the healthy foundation he'd built.

Why? Because somewhere deep down in the basement of his brain, he still didn't believe he deserved to be happy.

Over time, with the support of his counselor and a terrifying leap of faith, Kenny learned how to believe otherwise and started to build the necessary tools to help cope with such feelings.

Shortly after, he'd decided to take a chance and return to a lifelong passion. He accepted an assistant coaching position on the varsity football team at a nearby high school.

And then he'd asked Sarah to start attending counseling with him.

After much deliberation, she accepted and, as time passed, they began to repair the damage he'd done to their relationship. For Kenny, it'd felt like the start of yet another unexpected journey in life, and he'd been filled with gratitude that he didn't have to make such an arduous trip alone. On a daily basis, he was amazed by Sarah's compassion and understanding, her ability to forgive and trust again.

Four months later, she moved back into the apartment.

A year after that, they bought their condo by the river.

Kenny wiped his eyes and got up from the sofa. He turned off the television and looked around the family room. He stared at the photographs sitting on the mantle above the fireplace and the family portrait hanging on the wall. He owed everything he had—and everything he was—to Sarah. He couldn't imagine life without her.

At that moment, standing there in the dark, he promised himself he wasn't going to let anything get in the way of their happiness.

✳

SARAH WOKE UP and was instantly aware that she was alone in bed. She rolled over and looked at the alarm clock on the end table: 12:33 a.m. *Another late game? Or had Kenny fallen asleep on the sofa?*

She knew she'd been hard on him earlier, but she didn't know what else to do. The news had felt like a slap to the face. In her heart, she trusted Kenny...but she was also afraid. A part of her would probably always be afraid.

She was about to get up and go to the bathroom when she heard the inside door to the garage open and close downstairs. *That's odd,* she thought.

And then she heard footsteps crossing the kitchen into the foyer and heading up the stairway. *Had Kenny gone somewhere? Where could he have possibly been this late?*

Her heart started pounding in her chest.

Why don't you ask him?

Kenny crept into the bedroom, trying to be quiet, and tip-toed to the bathroom. He eased the door closed and turned on the light.

You're scared to ask him, aren't you?

Sarah rolled over.

Oh, shut up.

When Kenny emerged from the bathroom a few minutes later, she pretended to be asleep.

FRIDAY

KENNY WAS explaining a new blitz package to the starting defense when his cellphone buzzed in his pocket. Normally, he would never touch his phone during practice, but nothing about the past week had been remotely normal. He slid the phone out of his sweatshirt and squinted in the glare of the afternoon sun to read the screen: SARAH HOME.

"Take five and get some water," he told the boys. They headed for the sideline.

He pressed ACCEPT CALL.

"Hello?"

"I need you to come home, Kenny."

"What's wrong?"

Her voice dropped. "The detectives are here. Both of them."

Kenny's mouth went dry.

"They say what they want?"

"Not yet. I told them I wouldn't talk until you got here. Can you come?"

Kenny scanned the opposite end of the practice field, spotted Coach Mezzanotte down on a knee, talking to his quarterback. "I'll tell Dom it's an emergency. Give me fifteen."

ᴇᴌᴌ⁓

KENNY WALKED IN the door twenty minutes later and found Sarah waiting in the living room with the two detectives. Detective Jenkins was sitting in his favorite reading chair, leaning over and scratching Bandit behind the ears. Bandit wagged his tail and arched his furry back in a shameful display of outright betrayal. Kenny's first impulse was to tell the detective to get her damn hands off his dog, but he managed to resist.

"Sorry to keep you all waiting," he said, sitting next to Sarah on the sofa. "Traffic was horrible."

"No problem," Detective Jenkins said. "We've had a very nice conversation while we waited."

"You have?" Kenny asked, looking at Sarah with surprise.

"Detective Jenkins has a daughter Natalie's age and Detective Giambanco has a son a year older."

"We've been comparing notes," Detective Jenkins said, smiling.

Kenny couldn't remember if he'd ever seen the detective smile before. He didn't think so. He hoped it was a good sign. "So did the three of you come up with anything interesting?"

"Only that I'm glad I have a son," Detective Giambanco said. "Teenaged girls sound like a handful."

They all laughed and then Sarah put an abrupt end to the good feelings in the room: "Now that my husband is here, I'd like for you to tell us why you've come today."

Detective Jenkins nodded. "Back to business, Mrs. Tucker."

"I'm afraid so," Sarah said, softening her voice. "Natalie will be finished with tutoring soon. I'm hoping we can wrap it up before she gets home."

"We came to tell you two things," Detective Jenkins said, looking from Sarah to Kenny. She gestured for her partner to continue.

"Early this morning, two men fishing in Lake Codorus discovered a woman's body floating in a shallow lagoon at the north end of the lake."

Sarah reached over and squeezed Kenny's knee so hard he flinched. He took her hand and held it.

"The woman was nude and severely beaten. We're still waiting on the M.E. for an official cause of death, but the woman also suffered a number of stab wounds." He glanced at his partner. "Any of them could have been life-threatening."

"Is it her?" Sarah asked.

"The woman's fingers had been cut off so we were unable to check for prints," Detective Giambanco continued. "But we were able to get a positive ID from two family members."

"The victim is Katherine Morris, the woman from the video," Detective Jenkins said.

Sarah made a choking noise in the back of her throat.

"Are you okay, Mrs. Tucker?" Detective Giambanco asked.

"I don't know," she managed. "All I can think is I wish we'd heard her on the porch that night. I wish we'd been able to save her."

"You said you had two things to tell us?" Kenny asked.

Detective Giambanco nodded. "We also wanted to give you a heads-up that we'll be conducting a preliminary search of Tom Carpenter's residence this evening."

Kenny sat back on the sofa. "Jesus."

"That's ridiculous," Sarah said, shaking her head. "Tom didn't do anything."

"You could be right, Mrs. Tucker," Detective Jenkins said. "But we've received a handful of tips that we've deemed worthy of following up so that's what we're doing."

"Before I forget," Detective Giambanco said. "Have you been at home every night this week, Mr. Tucker?"

Kenny tried to match the detective's stare and couldn't. "I was out with friends for a while on Wednesday night. Right here in the neighborhood. I can give you their names if you'd like. You've already talked to a couple of them."

"That would probably be a good idea."

"Why are you asking?" Sarah said, her voice edged with panic.

Kenny leaned forward. "Am I a suspect?"

"We're just making sure we have all our bases covered," Detective Giambanco said.

"So Wednesday night?" Detective Jenkins asked. "You were home the rest of the week?"

"Yes," Kenny said, struggling to remain calm. "I was right here the other nights."

"Well, we appreciate your time, Mr. and Mrs. Tucker." Both detectives stood up. "I'd like to get those names and then we'll be on our way."

Sarah watched Detective Jenkins write down the names of Kenny's four best friends in the world—and tried very hard not to think about the previous night when she'd heard the garage door open and close shortly after midnight.

~~~

NATALIE KICKED OFF her black-and-white checkered Vans, plugged her iPhone into the wall charger and flopped on top of her bed. She rolled onto her stomach and tapped the SNAPCHAT icon on the screen of her phone. She opened the Group Chat for Madison, Krissy, and Taylor, and started typing:

NAT: Just got home from tutoring.

Five seconds later—

MAD: bout time, girl. Wyd

NAT: Getting ready to eat dinner. U?

MAD: just ate

TAYLOR: me2

MAD: what time u coming over

TAYLOR: soon as my sis gets home

NAT: Don't think I'm gonna. My parents are being so moody and weird it's not worth the hassle.

MAD: wtf

KRISSY: wtf

NAT: I know.

MAD: just come will be so much fun

KRISSY: yeah don't be a loserrrrrr

NAT: I wanna but my mom said if I stay the night she has to talk to all of your moms first and I'm not allowed to go outside or anywhere else and I have to call her and check in and she'd have to pick me up early in the morning blah blah blah

MAD: told u not to tell em about the cutie in the car. he was just tryna pick u up babe

NAT: Maybe.

TAYLOR: what else was he gonna do kidnap u?

NAT: Not funny

KRISSY: heard one of the detectives is a hottie

NAT: Ewwww.

TAYLOR: lol

NAT: Who told u that?

KRISSY: my mom!

NAT: Double ewwwwww

KRISSY: ikr

TAYLOR: your mom is dope

MAD: so u comin or what

NAT: I don't think so. Maybe next weekend will be better.

MAD: blah blah blah

TAYLOR: zzzzzzzzzzz

KRISSY: shane gonna be bummed u didn't come

NAT: Why you say that?

MAD: cuz I told him and bryan we were having a sleepover and they were gonna try to stop by

NAT: Your mom will never let them!!!

MAD: what she don't know won't hurt her I told them to come to basement window

NAT: OMG

TAYLOR: U should sneak out, nat!

KRISSY: yesssssss

MAD: yasssssss

TAYLOR: wait til your mom & dad are sleepin and come over!

NAT: Ummm doubt that would work.

TAYLOR: why not? my dad's so hammered by 10 I could do cartwheels outta the door and he wouldnt notice

NAT: My father doesn't drink.

TAYLOR: oh yeah

MAD: bummer

NAT: I'm gonna go eat now. Snap me later.

KRISSY: we'll send you a pic of shane

NAT: Is he really coming over?

TAYLOR: that's what Bryan said

NAT: They probably won't

KRISSY: they might

TAYLOR: sneak out!

MAD: sneak out!

KRISSY: sneak out!

NAT: lol

Natalie clicked out of the Group Chat. She rolled onto her back and stared at the ceiling. *I'd be crazy to even think about sneaking out, wouldn't I? Wouldn't I?*

She got up from the bed and looked out her window into the back yard. *If she got caught, she'd be grounded for the rest of her life. Which was why she hadn't told her parents about the man she thought she'd seen following her on at least three different occasions now. The first time had been at dinner with her parents last weekend. The second had been after school two days ago while she'd been waiting outside of the cafeteria for her mom to pick her up. The most recent had been earlier this afternoon after tutoring. She knew it hadn't been her imagination all these times, but she also knew if she said anything to her parents, they would call the detectives again and she'd be stuck inside the house for the rest of the school year. Maybe forever.*

No way am I going to let that happen, Natalie thought, as she went downstairs for dinner.

⁂

"WHAT'S SARAH UP to?"

Kenny and Paul were sitting on the older man's porch, glasses of iced tea resting on the arms of their chairs. Paul was smoking his pipe, the spicy aroma reminding Kenny of his grandfather, one of the few pleasant memories he had of the man. Across the street, two sheriff's cruisers and the detectives' unmarked sedan were parked along the curb in front of Tom Carpenter's house. A crime lab van had pulled into the driveway a couple hours earlier.

"Watching a movie with Natalie," Kenny said. "She was a mess after the detectives left."

"They have anything else interesting to say?"

Kenny remembered his promise to keep the information confidential. "Not really. Mainly just wanted to let us know they were going to search Tom's house."

Paul took a drink of tea and gave his neighbor a look. "They told you to keep the rest of it under wraps, huh?"

"The rest of what under wraps?" Kenny said, trying to play dumb.

Paul winked at him. "Can't fool an old cop."

A uniformed policeman emerged from Tom Carpenter's front door, carrying several cardboard boxes stacked on top of each other. Detective Giambanco appeared right behind him, a large plastic bag dangling from his hand. Both men were wearing what looked like latex gloves.

"They've been in there a long time," Kenny said.

"Painstaking work. Gotta follow proper protocol to keep the chain of evidence intact."

"You really think they'll find anything?"

Paul shrugged. "Who knows? I like Tom a lot, but people never fail to surprise me."

"You mean disappoint you."

"That too," Paul said, nodding.

"Tom doesn't seem like the type to have a dark side," Kenny said. "He seems so…sedate."

Paul took a puff on his pipe, watched the smoke curl in between the porch railings and drift into the front yard. When he spoke again, his voice was tinged with sadness. "I think most everyone has a dark side. Just a matter of how deep it cuts and whether or not they're able to control it."

"Everyone?" Kenny asked.

Paul nodded, a faraway look in his eyes.

"That's pretty damn pessimistic."

"You think?"

"I do." Kenny shrugged. "I prefer to think that there are plenty of good people still walking around out there."

"Who said anything about good or bad? Lots of fine folks out there, present company included."

"So you're saying even the good ones have a dark side?"

"Many of them, yes."

"Explain."

"Take those buddies of yours, for example. Known each other most of your lives and the five of you would take a bullet for each other. You guys are the real deal, no doubt about it. But who knows what those fellows might do when no one else is looking. One might cheat at golf, another on his taxes, still another on his wife."

"Come on, the golf thing's not so bad, is it? Doesn't really count as a dark side."

"No?" Paul said, arching his eyebrows. "Part of me thinks it might all be connected."

"How so?" Kenny asked, uncrossing his legs and leaning forward in the chair.

"I can't even begin to tell you how many people I've arrested over the years who all claim essentially the same thing: I didn't mean to run him off the road, officer, I just snapped; I didn't mean to hit her so hard, I just snapped; I didn't mean to pull the trigger, I just lost my temper and snapped."

"You're talking about impulse crimes?"

Paul snapped his fingers. "But where do those impulses come from, Kenny? That's my point. We *all* have them. Somewhere. For most of us, they're buried beneath our good manners and civilized behavior and fancy iPhones, and it takes a moment of extreme duress to drag them anywhere near the surface. And when it happens, it's only for a flicker of time and then it's back to normal again. But for others..." He trailed off.

"For others?"

Paul's eyes narrowed. "It lives closer to the surface, and it's there every day. And instead of fighting it, they learn to *embrace* it."

"I knew guys like that back when I was drinking," Kenny said. "Dark hearts. Always looking for trouble."

Nodding. "And then there's the truly evil. The worst of them...they *listen* for it. All their lives. I really believe that."

"Listen for what?

"The *itch*...the *urge*...that tantalizing, hypnotizing, deceitful voice from somewhere underneath it all."

Kenny exhaled, pushing away the hazy memories of a different life, a different person. He slowly rose to his feet. "Think I'm going to head home and see if the girls left me any popcorn."

"Don't be a stranger."

"Right back atcha." He stepped off the porch and started across the lawn.

"Hey, Kenny?"

He stopped and turned around. "Yeah?"

"Don't pay any mind to my rambling. I'm just an old fool. I get in one of those blue moods of mine and I act like the sky's falling."

Kenny smiled. "Why don't you come over and watch a movie? Sarah and Nat would love that."

"Another night," Paul said, getting to his feet. "Think I'll tinker around in the basement for a spell. Get my mind off things."

⁓

"HOW'S THE MOVIE?" Kenny asked, walking into the family room.

Sarah and Natalie were cuddled beneath a blanket on the sofa, a bowl of popcorn nestled between them. The lights were turned off.

"Sooo dumb," Natalie said.

Sarah tossed a kernel of popcorn at the teenager. "It is not. It's sweet."

Natalie rolled her eyes, picked up the popcorn from her lap and plopped it in her mouth.

Kenny laughed. He was grateful she had decided to stay home tonight instead of going to Madison's for a sleepover. It'd been just what Sarah had needed. He grabbed his keys from the coffee table.

"Where are you going?" Sarah asked, suddenly on edge.

"I need to run to school real quick. I was in such a hurry when I left practice I forgot my laptop in the coaches' office."

"Don't they lock it when they leave?"

Kenny nodded. "They do, but a lot of people have a key to that door. Custodians, rent-a-cops, other coaches. I'd rather not take a chance with it being a weekend."

"The movie's almost over," she said. "Want me to go with you?"

"Nah, you girls relax. I'll be back before you know it." He headed for the door.

"Kenny?"

He turned around and looked at his wife. He recognized the expression on her face: she was worried—and suspicious.

"Be careful."

Kenny blew her a kiss and walked out the door.

THE MAN SLAMMED the bat against the wall, sending up a shower of concrete chips. His face contorted with rage, the veins in his forehead and neck bulging. *They're getting closer. Every day. They must've found the body.*

He moaned and swung the bat again and again, bashing the wall until he couldn't lift his arms anymore and his cheeks were coated in a gritty gray film of concrete dust. He flung the bat away in disgust and lifted his eyes to the ceiling—and howled with fury. He sounded more like an animal than a man. Thick ropes of saliva hung from the corners of his mouth. His nose was bleeding and his dark eyes, huge and bloodshot, darted nervously around the room. He started frantically pacing in a tight circle, mumbling to himself.

A cellphone rang.

The man abruptly stopped pacing, stood perfectly still, his head cocked to the side.

The phone rang again.

He blinked his eyes and slowly looked around the room, as if awakening from the depths of a deep dream.

The phone rang a third time.

The man pulled a cellphone from his pants pocket and stared at the screen—and smiled.

He lifted the phone to his ear.

"Hello," he said in an eerily calm voice.

He listened for a moment—and laughed.

"Sounds good to me. I'll see you in fifteen."

The man ended the call and returned the phone to his pocket. He wiped his mouth and nose with his shirtsleeve and slowly climbed the stairs. Before he closed the door behind him, the man turned off the basement lights.

SATURDAY

KENNY AND Sarah sat at the breakfast nook—their waffles and bacon growing cold on the table in front of them—and stared at the small television on the kitchen counter.

A photograph of a young smiling Katherine Morris replaced the Lake Codorus shoreline in the upper left-hand corner of the screen. The Channel Two newscaster, movie-star handsome despite his caterpillar eyebrows, did his professional best to appear somber as he read from the teleprompter:

"...found by local fishermen early yesterday morning has been identified as twenty-eight-year-old Katherine Anne Morris of Baltimore, Maryland. A spokesperson for the Hanover County Medical Examiner's office reports that Morris had been beaten and stabbed to death approximately twelve to eighteen hours before she'd been abandoned in the water."

Grainy nighttime video footage of the Tuckers' front porch flashed on the screen, replacing Katherine Morris's once happy countenance. As the older, unsmiling Morris fruitlessly pressed the doorbell, the news anchor continued:

"…unfortunately serves as a sad final chapter to the mystery of The Girl on the Porch. If you have any additional information about Katherine Morris, please contact the Hanover County Sheriff's office at…"

Sarah turned off the television.

"What'd you do—?" Kenny stopped himself from finishing the question.

Sarah picked up her fork and ate a bite of cold waffle. She looked at her husband. "We already know how the story ends."

⌇

THE MAN PACED back and forth inside the garage. Furiously clenching and unclenching his fists. They had found the body. It was all over the news. He wanted to break something. He wanted to cut something. But he couldn't right now. He had places to be today and his absence would be noted.

He bit his lip until he tasted blood. He bit harder and swallowed. Then he walked outside and got into his car and drove away.

⌇

NATALIE AND MADISON stood in line at the concession stand, both of them busy on their cellphones. The score was tied at halftime, but neither of them had paid much attention to the game. Madison spent most of the first two quarters flirting with Tommy Noel, a cute eighth grader with a Justin Bieber haircut, and posting silly videos to TikTok. Natalie was in a crummy mood, and she wasn't entirely sure why. It might have been because she was so sick and tired of her mom and dad babying her. Ever since that strange woman had appeared on their front porch, it felt like Natalie was being held prisoner inside her house. In fact, today's football game was the first time she'd experienced a little freedom in nearly a week, and even then she had to text her mother every thirty minutes to let her know she was okay. Natalie's bad mood might also have been because Brian Thompkins had ignored her earlier when she'd said hi to him at the front gate. *Why were boys like that?* Natalie wondered. *They'd flood your phones with texts and snaps from the minute they woke up to the minute they went to sleep, but actually talking in person—especially in front of their friends—was somehow too much to ask.*

The line moved slowly forward, but neither of the girls noticed.

THE MAN STOOD amongst the crowd on the bleachers and used his cellphone to take another photo of the pretty teenager in line at the concession stand. He could feel his heart thumping in his chest. His fingertips were tingling. He lowered the phone and studied the girl's image on the screen. Sweet Natalie. She was perfect.

The man knew it was almost time to leave. They'd found the body. They were getting close.

But not yet, he thought, storing the photos in a hidden file. *Not yet.*

"WELL, THAT WAS fun," Sarah said.

The three of them were walking across the Harford Day School stadium parking lot. It was only two-thirty in the afternoon, but autumn clouds were gathering on the horizon and the light was already bleeding out of the sky. A cool breeze scattered fallen leaves across the asphalt and the rich smell of the pre-game bonfire still lingered in the air.

Natalie clutched a *BEAT WINTER HILL!* sign in one hand and texted her friends with the other. Mom and Dad held hands and strolled several paces behind her in a rare moment of unbridled contentment. The last week had taken its toll on the entire family and this afternoon's football game had been a welcome respite.

A carload of students cruised past, windows down, radio blaring. A teenage boy hung out the passenger window and waved. "Great game, Coach Tucker! Go Rams!" The driver blew the horn.

Kenny gave the boy a thumbs up and shouted, "Put your seatbelt on, Henry!"

Two more cars drove past, blasting their horns.

"Sheesh," Natalie said, covering her ears. "You'd think we won the Super Bowl or something."

"We sort of did," her father said earnestly. "Winter Hill has won the conference four years in a row."

Sarah squeezed his hand. "I'm so proud of you."

"Be proud of the boys. They did all the hard work."

"I think we should cook out tonight and celebrate. Invite some friends over."

Kenny looked at her. Company was the last thing he wanted; he was exhausted, body and soul. "If that'll make you happy, let's do it."

Sarah beamed. "It'll be good for us. Get our minds off everything."

"Can Madison come over?" Natalie asked.

"You just spent the last three hours together," Sarah said.

Kenny made a face. "Only if she promises not to talk about aliens."

Natalie rolled her eyes. "Dad…"

"Fine. Ask her."

The girl started tapping away on her phone again.

"You relax the rest of the afternoon," Sarah said, as they reached the car. "I'll run to the grocery store and handle all the preparations."

Kenny smiled at his wife. "I'm sure not going to argue with that."

He unlocked the car and swung open the driver's door. He was about to climb inside when he noticed the folded piece of paper tucked underneath the windshield wiper. He quickly reached around and grabbed it. Glancing at it just long enough to confirm it was another one of the DO YOU KNOW THIS WOMAN? flyers, he crumpled the paper into a ball and stuffed in into his pants pocket.

"What was that?" Sarah asked, as they slipped on their seatbelts.

"What was what?"

"The paper on the windshield," she said, looking at him closely.

"Oh, that." He shrugged and started the engine. "It was nothing. An advertisement for a furniture sale."

Sarah glanced around at the remaining cars as they pulled out of the parking lot. She didn't see a single windshield with a sales flyer on it. She stared at her husband as he drove. *Why was he lying to her? What was he hiding?*

THERE WERE NINE of them on the back patio: Kenny and Sarah, Angie and Frank, Trey and Carly, Ian and Katy, and Paul from next door. Kenny was grilling burgers and dogs and barbeque chicken. Sarah was pouring the wine, and Ian and Trey had brought over two coolers filled with beer, soda, and Gatorade. Natalie and Madison and the other children—six of them in all; four girls and two boys—were playing Kan Jam in the back yard. Bandit was prowling under the patio table for scraps.

"I knew it was him all along," Angie said.

"Then why haven't the police arrested him yet?" Ian asked.

They all looked at Paul—the resident expert.

He finished chewing a bite of hot dog. "Could be they're waiting on a piece of evidence they sent out for testing. Or they need to interview another witness. Or he could be innocent."

"Innocent my ass," Frank said.

Kenny bristled. "Tom's never done a damn thing to any of us."

"Too bad Katherine Morris can't say the same thing," Frank said, draining his beer.

"What's your problem, Frank? You jealous or something?"

"Jealous of Tom?" His face flushed red. "What the hell's that supposed to mean?"

"Can we just change the subject?" Sarah asked, leaning across the table to refill Carly's wine glass.

"I think that's a good idea," Paul said mildly.

Kenny opened the lid to the grill and started flipping burgers. Sarah eased up next to him. "Easy tiger," she whispered.

"I'm sick of him. Always running his mouth about stuff he knows nothing about."

"I'm with you, but let's save the fireworks for later when we're alone." She squeezed his arm and walked back to the ladies.

"Who wants a burger?" Kenny asked, trying to sound pleasant. Inside, he was still steaming.

Katy raised her hand. "Yes, please."

"Anyone else?"

"I'll take one," Trey said.

Kenny yelled down to the kids. No one answered. He tried again. Nothing.

"It's like talking to the trees," he said, shaking his head.

"Just be grateful they're not staring at their phones for a change," Trey said.

Sarah pointed a finger at him. "Bingo."

Kenny was about to try the kids for a third and final time when his cellphone buzzed in his pocket. He slid it out, checked the screen, and answered.

"Hello—"

"Don't say anything," the voice on the other end instructed. "Just listen very carefully."

"Okay."

"You're in the back yard on the patio, is that correct?"

"That's right."

His voice didn't sound like his own.

"And Trey Whiteford is there with you?"

His heart skipped a beat.

"Yes."

Sarah was looking at him funny now.

"Is there any chance he's armed?"

Kenny glanced at his friend, quickly looked away. "I don't think so."

"I'm sorry, Mr. Tucker," Detective Jenkins said and hung up the phone.

Kenny tapped the END CALL button and was still staring at the screen in a daze when they heard cars screeching to a stop in the street in front of the house.

Everyone turned and listened.

"What's that?" Natalie asked, looking up at the adults on the patio.

Frank shot to his feet, shouting, "I told you! I told you it was him!"

"Are you okay?" Sarah asked, coming up beside Kenny. "Who was that?"

A cacophony of muffled voices and footfalls and radio chatter came from the direction of the driveway.

Kenny looked at his wife and opened his mouth—but no words would come out.

"Kenny?" she said, scared now, shaking him by the shoulder.

The back gate crashed open. Uniformed police officers swarmed into the yard.

"Everybody freeze!"

Men with guns wearing black helmets and body armor hurdled the fence on the opposite side of the house.

"Nobody move! Nobody move!"

Kenny wrapped his arms around his wife and pulled her close to his chest.

"Hands up! Lemme see your hands!"

In the back yard, Natalie knelt in the grass, fingers laced behind her head. Madison and the other girls were crying, and the smaller of the two boys had a dark stain spreading on the front of his pants and was calling for his mom.

"Natalie!" Sarah pushed her husband away and started down the patio stairs.

"Not another step!" an officer dressed all in black ordered, leveling an assault rifle at Sarah's chest.

"Please listen to him, Sarah," Paul said from directly behind her.

She slowly backed up the stairs and turned to look at the others. They all had their hands in the air. Even Paul. Their pale faces appeared stunned and terrified—except for Trey. He looked furious. Face flushed and jaw clenched, his eyes were like daggers, despite the three guns pointed at him from inches away.

Detective Jenkins climbed the patio stairs, her partner a step behind, both grim-faced and armed.

"Trey Whiteford, you're under arrest for first-degree murder and unlawful felony imprisonment," Detective Jenkins said. A uniformed officer pulled Trey's arms behind his back and handcuffed him.

"Whaaat?" Carly cried out, reaching for her husband's arm.

A second officer stepped in and pushed her hand away.

"You have the right to remain silent," Detective Giambanco said. "Anything you say can and will be used against you in a court of law. You have the right to an attorney. If you cannot—"

"You're making a mistake," Trey said, and Sarah was astonished to see that he was smiling. The rage she had witnessed just seconds earlier was gone.

"If you say so," Detective Jenkins said, her stony expression unchanged.

"A big mistake," Ian said loudly. "Don't say another word, Trey. Not until you have a lawyer."

Carly sobbed and struggled to get to her husband. A female officer blocked her way and gently held her back.

"Get her outta here," Detective Giambanco ordered, and the female officer walked her down the stairs toward the back gate.

"Where are they taking her?" Sarah asked.

"Him too," Detective Giambanco said, not even trying to hide his disgust. A pair of officers stepped forward and escorted Trey off the patio.

"I'll be out by tomorrow morning," Trey called over his shoulder.

"I don't think so," Detective Jenkins said, gesturing for the officers to stop. "We executed a search warrant on 1912 Langston Drive this afternoon."

The corners of Trey's mouth twitched.

"The Wilkerson House?" Kenny asked.

"We stumbled across some pretty interesting items in the basement."

Trey's jaw began to tremble.

"We also searched the cabin your uncle left you in his estate three years ago."

Trey nostrils flared and he cocked his head to the side, like he was listening to a voice the rest of them couldn't hear.

"What cabin?" Ian asked. He looked over at Kenny. "You know anything about a cabin?"

The detective waved a hand at the officers. "You can take him—"

Trey erupted, bellowing like a wild animal that had been dealt a fatal wound, and lunged up the stairs at the detective, dragging the two uniformed officers along with him. Teeth bared, spittle flying, he no longer resembled the man Kenny had known for most of his life.

Detective Jenkins calmly pivoted to the side, swung her arm hard across her body, and pistol-whipped Trey Whiteford in the center of his forehead. He went down in a heap.

"Get him out of my sight," she said.

The two officers picked up the unconscious man and carried him out of the back yard.

Sarah stared at the detective in shock and asked in quiet voice: "Can I hug my daughter now?"

Detective Jenkins nodded at the officer standing in Sarah's way and walked away.

KENNY STARED OUT the bedroom window at the dark street below. The last of the news crews had packed up and left twenty minutes earlier, the handful of straggling neighbors not long after, like moths abandoning a burned-out light bulb. The weather forecast called for unseasonably chilly temperatures and overnight rain. The breeze had picked up, gusting fallen leaves across the lawn like tiny, swirling ghosts.

"You coming to bed?" Sarah asked, resting a hand on his shoulder.

Kenny nodded. "Soon."

"You okay?"

"No." He turned to her. "Are you?"

She shook her head. "No."

He wrapped his arms around her and closed his eyes—and said a silent thank you to whatever God existed in the stars above that Sarah had saved him.

"I keep thinking about Carly," Sarah said. "Do you know he's the only man she's ever been with? No boyfriends when she was younger, no freshman flings in college, not even a goodnight kiss."

Kenny took a deep breath. "I don't even know what to say to her."

"She never mentioned to me that she was away at her sister's the night Katherine Morris came to our house, but even if she had, I wouldn't have given it a second thought. I mean…it's Trey we're talking about."

"I've known him since we were in little league. Twelve years old."

"Do you…really think he did it?"

Kenny didn't say anything for a long time. When he finally did, his voice was filled with sadness.

"Detective Jenkins is very good at her job and she told me they have enough evidence to put him away for the rest of his life."

"Did she say anything else?"

Kenny closed his eyes again. "She said Katherine Morris wasn't the only one."

"The only what?" Sarah asked. "Wait a minute, you mean—"

"Let me finish," Kenny said. "I can only do this once."

Squeezing his hand. "Okay."

"They have evidence of other victims. In other places. Spanning a number of years. Trey drugged them and raped them and killed them. And he kept souvenirs. They found everything."

Sarah was crying now, her hand over her mouth.

"He was getting ready to run. Maybe even tonight. They found cash and a fake passport at the Wilkerson house. He knew the police were getting close."

"I still…can't believe it."

"It'll be all over the news by tomorrow. Detective Jenkins wanted me to hear it from her first."

"How is this…even possible?"

Kenny shook his head. "He had a lot of secrets. There were sexual harassment accusations in college. Official charges were never brought, but whatever happened was enough for him to get kicked out of his fraternity."

"Detective Jenkins told you this?"

He nodded. "And there were rumors at work. That he was fooling around on Carly. Sometimes, he came into the office with scratches on his arms and face. I'd noticed them before, but he always said he got from playing rugby."

Tears streamed down her face. "Why would he…?"

"I don't know, honey. Paul told me once that some people have urges…who knows where they come from…and instead of fighting it, they embrace it." He looked at his wife. "I just don't know."

"Come to bed, baby." Sarah touched his arm. "Come to bed."

"Soon," he said. "I have to call the guys first."

"Oh, Kenny." Her heart breaking into a million tiny pieces.

"They shouldn't hear it from anyone else."

"I'll stay with you if you want."

He shook his head. Kissed her on the cheek. "My phone's downstairs in the kitchen. Go to bed. I'll be up soon."

"I'll be waiting."

Kenny headed for the hallway, stopped at the door and turned around. "Thank you for loving me, Sarah."

A sob escaped her throat. "Thank you for loving me back."

He walked down the hall, thinking about the other things Detective Jenkins had told him, details he would never share with Sarah for as long as he drew breath, or with anyone else for that matter—the series of sadistic, taunting letters the police had received over the past decade (all written on an old manual typewriter, which was found during their search of the Whiteford residence), the more than a dozen glossy photographs of unidentified women they'd discovered under the floorboards of the isolated cabin, and the countless photos of Natalie they'd found hidden on Trey's cellphone.

Kenny paused and nudged open the door to his daughter's bedroom. He peeked his head inside and watched the steady rise and fall of the blanket she was sleeping beneath—and then he closed the door and went downstairs to call his friends.

RICHARD CHIZMAR is the *New York Times* bestselling author of the *Gwendy Trilogy* (with Stephen King), as well as *Chasing the Boogeyman, Widow's Point*, and many other books. *Becoming the Boogeyman* will be published by Simon & Schuster/Gallery Books in October.

He is the founder/publisher of *Cemetery Dance* magazine and the Cemetery Dance Publications book imprint. He has edited more than 35 anthologies and his short fiction has appeared in dozens of publications, including multiple editions of *Ellery Queen's Mystery Magazine* and *The Year's 25 Finest Crime and Mystery Stories*. He has won two World Fantasy awards, four International Horror Guild awards, and the HWA's Board of Trustee's award.

Chizmar (in collaboration with Johnathon Schaech) has also written screenplays and teleplays for United Artists, Sony Screen Gems, Lions Gate, Showtime, NBC, and many other companies. He has adapted the works of many best-selling authors including Stephen King, Peter Straub, and Bentley Little.

Chizmar's work has been translated into more than fifteen languages throughout the world, and he has appeared at numerous conferences as a writing instructor, guest speaker, panelist, and guest of honor.